Hidden Agendas

Autumn Flowers

DEDICATION

I would like to dedicate this book to my dear friend, Florence Manuel, may she rest in peace. She was always there encouraging me as I wrote this novel. Much love Florence, you are sorely missed.

TABLE OF CONTENTS

Read Between the Lies

Bruised, broken and burned.

My heart buried in the wreckage.

Pain and despair were my lessons learned.

Notions of being in love holding me hostage.

Always alone in my thoughts.

Forever haunted by my past.

Yet through the suffering, I fought and fought.

Like a Phoenix, I rose from the ash.

There is beauty in my struggle, from the flames I rise.

Now, with a fire in my soul, I learn to fly high.

I charge forward with only one rule in mind.

The only way to guard your heart is to read between the lies.

Autumn Flowers

ACKNOWLEDGMENTS

First and foremost, I would like to thank God for everything that he has done in my life. I give him all the praise and glory. I would like to thank my children, for giving me motivation to strive for excellence and to be the best example that I can be for them. To my oldest daughter, you have overcome so many obstacles and I am so proud of the woman that you are becoming. To my youngest daughter, you are wise beyond your years, continue keeping God first and you will achieve great things. I would like to thank my parents for their love and continued support. Mom, you taught me how to be a strong and independent woman, I only pray that I possess at least a fraction of the strength that you do. Dad, you taught me the importance of family. You have such a big heart, one that I love and admire. Thank you all for believing in me the way that you do. I love you all infinitely.

Autumn Flowers is a mother of two daughters before anything else. She currently resides in North Carolina. The novel *Hidden Agendas* marks the introduction of Autumn Flowers as an author. To learn more connect with her via:

Email: TheAutumnFlowers@gmail.com

Instagram: @The_Autumn_Flowers

Facebook: @theautumnflowers

LONELY

It has been three years since my last relationship and I vowed that I would never allow myself to be placed in a similar situation. That is, in an emotionally unhealthy and physically abusive relationship. My ex cheated on me, he was emotionally manipulative, neglectful and he was physically abusive. Instead of enduring that type of treatment again, I decided that I would remain single. Quite frankly, I was prepared to remain single forever because at the end of that relationship came a daughter that I now had to consider and be an example for. I was not going to bring different prospects around my daughter and I swore that I would never allow her to see me endure the treatment that her father put me through.

The first year was easy but as the time was ticking away, I was beginning to ask myself if I'd be a single forever. Would I never experience the feeling of "true love"? It was a feeling that so desperately wanted to experience. I felt that I deserved to experience that feeling of euphoria that I have only heard so much about. I wanted that love like Cliff and Claire Huxtable on 'The Cosby Show'. Claire was a sophisticated, driven, family-oriented woman and Cliff was a successful doctor who was also family oriented who faithfully supported his wife and children. Their love was pure and the commitment strong. Their love withstood the challenges that most relationships face. The type of love that is unconditional, supportive, and undying. You know, that Barack and Michelle Obama type of love where there was no doubt that the other had your back, no matter what.

The idea of commitment has become lost in translation in this day in age and it is difficult to find a love like that. In this you only live once (YOLO) day in age, the concept of commitment had become foreign. I had so much to offer, yet I was still searching for real love. I was what some would refer to as that 'ride or die' woman. The type that once I'm in it, I'm in it wholeheartedly and I would have your back through whatever. I was loyal to a fault because I had been all in for a man who did not reciprocate the loyalty, support and faithfulness. I did not know how to back out of a situation once I had put my all into it.

I began to question if I had been cursed or if I had done something awful in my lifetime to deserve this. I prayed and prayed for God to forgive me for whatever I had done to deserve this. I knew that I was a good person and I had many qualities that many suitable mates desire. I was beautiful, loyal, financially stable, educated, responsible, and most of all I was a great mother. So why was it that the relationship that I had been in had been so unsuccessful? What was it that I was doing wrong? These were questions that I had to have the answers to before I could think of entertaining another relationship.

It was difficult for me to see other happy couples, although I was extremely happy for them I was aching to experience that same feeling. As time passed, I grew less and less hopeful that I ever would. I resented the relationships where I saw that one person was this wholesome ideal mate and the other person in the relationship took that individual for granted. It was a concept that became increasingly prevalent and made me feel that all hope had been diminished, until the day that I met Jaiden.

Jaiden was not a tall man, but he was very handsome and there he stood in uniform, with a killer smile, bronze complexion, and he just had a presence about himself that was intriguing. In that sense, he was not the typical tall, dark and handsome type that everyone seems to seek but I did not have a specific physical type. The fact that he was in uniform was somewhat off putting because I had decided a long time ago that I would never date a military man. I grew up in a military town and had heard so many horror stories about how the relationships ended. It was something about him that looked so innocent and genuine.

I was standing in line at the grocery store and although I noticed him, I was too shy to say anything. We made eye contact, but I quickly put my head down to avoid his gaze. I could feel his hazel eyes looking at me and I was afraid to look up, but when I did he was standing right there, "good afternoon" he said respectfully. I was impressed with his approach. He was charming. It was a huge change from the men that approached me "Ayo, what's your name sexy?" or "Hey cutie, you got a man?" or some other lame ass line they come at you with to get your attention.

"Good afternoon. How are you?" I responded as I smiled back at him. I was extremely nervous, in part because

I did not know where this conversation would lead. Also, because I was very shy.

"My name is Jaiden, what is your name?" he said as he extended his hand out to shake my hand. He was in uniform, so his last name was on his jacket, Williams.

"My name is Alyssa, Alyssa Calloway, it is a pleasure to make your acquaintance" I said while blushing.

"Could I take you out for dinner sometime?" Jaiden asked charming me with his gorgeous smile. He did not waste any time and I thought that was a bit rushed considering the only piece of information that we shared with one another was our names. That smile of his made me forget my common sense in that moment. I suppose it was safe to say I was a sucker for a nice smile. I was hesitant to answer because generally the answer would have been emphatically "NO" but for some reason I did not want to decline an invitation with this perfect stranger. It felt as though when our eyes met there was an intense connection. I was intrigued by him. I wanted to know more, so I politely obliged his offer. We exchanged numbers, he said he would call me later and we parted ways in the store.

As I walked out the store, I was smiling and recalling our meeting in the grocery store. My mother always told that you do not find good men in the clubs or local bars, but they could be found in church and the grocery store. I was sure that I would not meet anyone at a club anymore considering that is where I had met my daughter's father Kareem. Kareem was also very charming, had a nice smile but he also had difficulties keeping steady employment, he had difficulty remaining faithful although I don't think he ever tried and he had difficulty telling the truth. I sold myself short when I remained in a relationship with him and I absolutely refused to be a fool again. I had to be careful. After all, I had another life to consider that would be affected by my decisions. I could not allow another man to come in and put on the charming routine and fall head over heels in love only to find out that it was just an act. I knew that part of my problem was that once I have fallen for a man, I am all in 100% committed and it is difficult for me to let go if things began to sour. It was important for me to be cautious but in a way, I did not trust myself.

I knew that I was eager to have this feeling of love fill my life and I did not want to allow my desires to override my acumen as it has in the past. The feeling of loneliness has a way of altering a person's better judgement. At the same time, I did not want my fear to prevent me from finding "true love". I wanted to believe that after three years of celibacy, that I had become secure in being alone instead of viewing it as loneliness but who was I fooling, I was ready to end that period in my life.

I walked into my mother's house to pick up my daughter. As soon as I entered the door my daughter Alexis came running into my arms, "mommy, I missed you" she screamed and gave me the biggest hug. My mother picked Alexis up from school every day because I did not get off work until after 5 o'clock, so my mother kept her until I came and got her to help me out. I was so thankful for my mother, she was retired so she had a lot of free time and she was always willing to spend time with her grandchild. It was such a huge help for me being a single parent. I had to save money where I could, and childcare was a great start. Besides that, it is difficult to trust strangers with your kids even in establishments such as daycares.

My mother looked at me as I hugged Alexis with a look of bewilderment. Apparently, she could see the look of excitement on my face. "Where have you been?" she asked with her head tilted to the side and a smirk on her face.

"I stopped by the store to pick up a few things to cook for dinner" I responded with a smile on my face.

"If I didn't know any better, I would say that you have met you someone special" my mother said. How could she quite possibly know that I had met anyone at all, I certainly did not tell her. I guess that is a gift that mothers have and I hoped that I could be as intuitive with my own daughter.

"I actually did meet someone, while I was at the store this evening."

My mother sat down and smiled at me "well, tell me more about him."

"He is a very handsome man. He has beautiful hazel eyes and a gorgeous smile. His name is Jaiden, he's in the Army. That is pretty much all I know about him right now. He asked to take me out to dinner and I said yes."

"Oh, so you have a date?"

"We have not set a date to go out, we just exchanged numbers. I am just going to wait on his call." I said in a nonchalant tone.

"Okay, try not to be too hard on him, you know how you can be" she said sarcastically. My mother was happy to learn that he was in the military yet shocked because she knew my position on military men. She wanted me to find happiness and she knew that I wanted to be a part of a family unit. Ever since I was a small child, I have only been truly committed to one thing, becoming a wife and mother. I wanted a loving, supportive, family unit of my own. In my young mind a career was important but not nearly as important as having a family. She knew that I was incredibly disappointed that things did not work out with Alexis' father.

I shared with my mother how nervous I was about going out with him. After all, it had been three years since I had even entertained the idea of dating. I was not sure why I was so ready and willing to go out with this man that I had just met. I met men all the time, but I never gave them the time of day. I would give out fake numbers or tell them that I didn't give out my number and I would take theirs never to call them. However, in all fairness, the way that these men approached me was a turn off. They either looked or acted high or drunk, came off as the player type, or approached me with a line like "Aye shorty, what's your name?" or "Hey cutie, let me get your number". I mean, is this how grown men approach grown women? There were a few that had also been as charming when they approached me, and I gave them my number but when they called, and we spoke on the phone there was a disconnect and we learned that we had absolutely nothing in common.

"Alyssa, all men are not the same. You have got to give someone a chance to be the man that you are looking for. He has a stable career, which is a good start, but you have to go out with him to find out if you are compatible."

She was right, I did not want to be lonely for the rest of my life. It was time to open myself up to someone and I deserved to be happy, but I did not want to get my hopes up with this guy that I just met.

As I walked back into my house with my daughter, my phone rings. To my surprise, it was Jaiden. My heart sank and began to beat rapidly. I felt butterflies in my stomach. Should I answer the phone or just let it ring? I decided to let it ring, I didn't want to seem too available and I had to get my little girl ready for bed. She had already eaten over my mother's house. I called him back once I had gotten Alexis settled in bed. The phone rang several times and I thought, *I should have just answered when he called because now he was not answering the phone.* Just as I was about to hang up, he answers "Hello."

"Hello, is this Jaiden Williams?

"Yes, speaking" he said.

"This is Alyssa, I-----".

"Yes, I know, I have your number saved in my phone. I was hoping that I would hear back from you tonight" he said anxiously.

"I was a little busy with my daughter when you called". I wanted to make him aware right away that it was not just me. Some men do not want to date a woman with kids and if he was that type of man, there was no sense in either of us wasting our time.

"So, you have a little girl, how old is she? He said with enthusiasm.

"She is five years old" I said proudly.

"I have a 9-year-old son who lives with me and a 10-year-old daughter who lives with her mother. I wish that my daughter stayed with me too, she is really not in a suitable environment, but she is a little girl who wanted desperately to live with her mother" he said.

"Wow.... I know how tough it is being a single parent" I replied.

"Yea, but I make a way and we do aight. My son JJ is currently staying with my mom. I just dropped him off over the weekend. I had to make some arrangements for him while I am deployed.

My heart sank, *if he is getting ready to deploy, what sense would it make for me to go out with him and spend time with him.* The wheels began to spin in my mind. I wondered if he was just trying to see how far he could go with me before he went off on deployment. I was not that type of woman, so if sex was what he was looking for, he would be sorely mistaken. "When will you be deploying and where to?" I asked.

"I will be leaving for Iraq in 3 weeks and I will be there for a year."

"Can I ask, why you would like to get to know me if you are getting ready to deploy so soon?"

"Honestly, the moment I saw you, I knew that I had to speak to you and I wanted to get to know you better. I simply did not want to let you get away."

I was touched by his response, but I still had reservations. We continued the conversation and we talked for hours on the phone. I learned so much about him and he learned a lot about me. We seemed to have an instant connection and we had so many things in common. He told me that he been married before and his ex-wife was a woman that he claimed did not want to work or do anything to better herself. She was uneducated and had no drive according to Jaiden. He explained the situation with his daughter and said that she had gone back to live with her mother about a year ago. Jaiden had a stable job, had custody of his son and he struck me as being very intelligent. He seemed perfect for me, but I was still quite hesitant to spend time with him just because I could not understand why he would want to pursue anything serious right before he deploys. I knew that men could be smooth talkers and that he could very well just be seeking someone to have a "good time" with before he leaves. I had my defenses up. We planned to go out for dinner the following day and I thought that was innocent enough. We would be in public place, there would be no pressure. After our long conversation the night before, I was really looking forward our 'first date'.

As time neared for our date, I grew increasingly nervous. I made some arrangements with my mother to keep my daughter a little later than usual so that I could meet up with Jaiden after work. We planned to go to dinner after work at Skyview, an upscale restaurant with a beautiful view of the city.

"What is this glow I see on you?" said Vanessa. Vanessa was a co-worker and friend that I had made since working there. Vanessa was the type of friend who did not have a filter, she said exactly what she was thinking. "You must have got you some last night, and why didn't I know that you had someone in your life?" she said with one hand on her hip as she studied my body language.

"I just met someone the other day and we are going out

tonight after work and no I did not give up these goodies". We both laughed.

"I am happy to see you getting out and enjoying yourself, it is about time". Vanessa knew about my past relationship and how I had been celibate for the past three years. She wanted me to just date and enjoy the company of a man and that is what I intended to do. Vanessa was someone that I not only shared a close working relationship with, but we spent time together outside of work. She was preparing for her wedding and I was going to be one of her bridesmaids. Vanessa was with the love her life. She and her man gave me hope that true love still existed. I admired the relationship that they shared; the communication, the affection, the understanding, and the loyalty.

Vanessa was about a year or so younger than me, but she was someone that I looked up to. I didn't have a lot of friends for the most part I kept to myself. I had been hurt not only in romantic relationships but in friendships as well. I was guarded; I did not allow people to get to close to me or for me to get too close to people. However, Vanessa was certainly someone that I considered a friend.

Later that evening, I pulled up to the restaurant where we had planned to meet at and I see him pull up right beside me. I get out of my car and I saw a new dark blue BMW 740 Li with chrome rims and dark tinted windows and all I could hear was bass. He parked and then stepped out of the vehicle. He was dressed in civilian clothes matching from head to toe; he was wearing Carolina blue shorts, Carolina blue shirt with dark blue stripes and Carolina blue and white J's. I was wearing a white sundress that flowed in the wind. We walked up to one another and hugged. He grabbed my hand and held it as we walked into the restaurant. The hostess found us seating in a small booth and we sat down and ordered our food. "Have you ever eaten here before?" he asked.

"Yes, I have, my favorite dish is the Tuscan Chicken."

"I think I will try that today." He ordered for both of us and proceeded to ask me questions to break the ice. We shared beautiful conversation, we laughed, he complimented me, we connected. For the first time since I met him, I started to feel as though I was in trouble. He was someone that I could fall for; but he was leaving soon. I was not interested in a long-distance relationship and I was not looking to simply have a casual sexual relationship either. I had never been in a long-distance relationship but if I were going to continue to see this man, it was the inevitable. At this point, I was intrigued as to where this could potentially go.

Once we decided to leave from the restaurant he asked if we could go to a nearby park. "I just do not want this night to end" he exclaimed. I agreed to go although I was skeptical, not because I felt uncomfortable, but I felt drawn to him and it was scaring me. I followed him to the park in my car. Once we arrived we both got out of our vehicles he walked towards me and grabs my hand. We walked hand in hand near the pond there at the park. It was beautiful, the sun was setting, and the sky had an orange hue. The sun was reflecting off the water. It was as if the sky was meeting the sun.   We stood there looking into one another's eyes and holding hands. *What is happening?* I thought to myself.

"Alyssa, I really do not want this night to end, I can see you as my wife" Jaiden said.

"Your wife?"   I said with a look of confusion.   If ever there was a moment where I became uncomfortable during our date, it was right then.   I mean who asks someone to marry them on the first date?   Well not ask per se but who even mentions the idea of marriage on the first date.   That seems like a red flag in my opinion.   At that moment, I felt that it was insincere, he could not really feel that he could see me as his wife.   Sounded like game to me.   I needed to get out of this situation, so I told him that I needed to leave to go and pick my daughter up.   He escorted me back to my car and once we reached my car, he looked me deep into my eyes and kissed my lips so tenderly.

He gently caressed my face and I felt butterflies in my stomach. "When can I meet your daughter?"

I was baffled by the question because I was not ready to bring him around my child.   "Ummm---I---I don't know, we will have to see how things go first.   I don't bring men around my daughter and I won't until I know that they are going to be around."

"I understand, I respect that."

"I am glad you understand."

I could not let him know that I had this warm and tingly feeling inside.   I simply got into my car and told him that I would see him soon.   As I drove away I thought long and hard about our evening together and how he had subtly or maybe not so subtly thought that I could be his ---wife. *Was he serious?* I thought to myself. *He couldn't be serious*, I chose to just pretend that he had not just said that instead of viewing his actions as a possible red flag. I have only heard about these types of things happening in the movies not in real life. However, I was delighted by the idea of a fairytale ending. Little did I know that I would soon learn that this was in fact a red flag to his hidden agenda.

PAST EXPERIENCE

I met Kareem when I was 19 years old fresh out of high school and I thought I knew everything about life. I was in my freshman year of college and I liked to go out and party with my college friends. I was newly independent, having moved out of my parent's house and I was eager to experience the world and all that it had to offer. While I would not say that I was wild, I would certainly say that enjoyed my youth and being carefree. I was young, energetic, beautiful and I had goals and aspirations. It didn't matter how much people told me to enjoy being young and not to worry about having a boyfriend, I still wanted one. Not just any boyfriend but someone that I could settle down with and build a family with down the road. I never wanted to be out there casually dating nor did I ever give myself the opportunity to do so. Besides that, I was focused on school and work and I did not have time to entertain foolishness. Throughout high school, I was the one that never had a boyfriend. Not because I was unattractive or could not pull one. It was more so because I realized that all the high school boys only wanted one thing and I simply was not interested.

I desired something meaningful and often I would get clowned for not wanting to play the field. It simply was not in my nature and I was unwilling to conform to the standards that my peers abided by although I respected their position.

I guess what they say "hindsight is always 20/20" held some weight because looking back I understand why they explored their options and I wished that I would have explored mine.

I had male friends and I hung out with them, but we never crossed any lines. In fact, at this point in my life, I had more male friends than I did female friends. Women just did not seem to understand me, nor did I understand them. In high school, girls thought I was bougie because I carried myself maturely and I was very articulate. The men recognized that and respected that about me because when they got to know me they realized that I was cool as a fan. It was easier for me to connect with men, but it was difficult to decipher who was trying to be my friend and who just wanted to get close to me for other nefarious reasons. I attracted the attention of a lot of men, but most were just not my type and did not spark that instantaneous connection that was sparked when I met Kareem. It was like I was drawn to him in some weird way. It was like we were two magnets facing one another, you could feel the electromagnetic pull.

Kareem approached me while my friends and I were at a fraternity party at a club, he was wearing a badge for a local radio station and I assumed that he worked there. He was a handsome guy, about 5'11", the complexion of Morris Chesnutt, a smile like Taye Diggs and a physique like The Roc. Cuts everywhere.

I could tell that he was older than me and that was a plus for me because I somehow saw that as a sign of maturity. I was looking for someone more mature than these other knuckle heads that simply wanted to get me in bed. "Hello there Gorgeous, how are you doing tonight?

"Fine thank you, how about yourself?"

"Yes, you are, what's a beautiful woman like you doing in a place like this?"

By this point, I was blushing "I was just hanging out with a few friends of mine. This place is full of beautiful women, why would you ask me that?"

"None of them as beautiful as you, what's ya name?

"Alyssa."

"Beautiful name for a beautiful woman."

"Thank you, you are not too bad yourself." I said as I laughed. He hit me with that smile and I could not help but blush. In that moment it felt as though we were the only ones in that club that night. We sat a table in the corner, he ordered drinks for us both and we talked and laughed all night. Although I was not of legal age to drink, I sipped on my beverage as if I were. I did not keep my age a secret though. He knew that I was just out of high school, but he also recognized that I was not like the average 19 almost 20-year-old woman. I had a sense of grace and maturity that was clearly visible even though I had a youthful appearance. I stood about 5'1", 130 lbs., long dark brown hair, caramel complexion, with curves in all the right places. I had often been compared with Nia Long from the movie 'Love Jones' except I was a little curvier. I had what they called an hour glass figure and every piece of clothing I wore fit me like a glove.

I had basically abandoned my friends who were there with me, to converse with him and in my mind, it was well worth it. My friends were sitting out in the car waiting for me, so we exchanged numbers and he said he would call me the following day. Sure enough, the following day my phone rang and it was him on the other end. I was delighted to hear his voice and to converse further with him. The attraction between us seemed so strong that it was hard to deny. We shared a connection and I was curious to see where things would go so when he asked to take me out, I happily obliged.

Kareem was a perfect gentleman when went out on our first date. He brought me a dozen beautiful red roses, he opened doors and pulled out my chair before I sat down. I did not even know that type of chivalry still existed. In an instant, he had swept me off my feet. I felt that warm and fuzzy feeling in my stomach when we talked on the phone and when we were together. We spent about three months dating before we engaged in a sexual relationship. In fact, I would not do anything with him until I knew that we were in a committed relationship. He was consistent in his actions during this time giving me zero red flags. Although, the fact that he was so perfect should have been one. He was everything that I had been searching for, tall, dark, handsome, respectful, generous, strong and attentive. We spent all of time together and we truly enjoyed each other's company.

BIRTHDAY SEX

One night, while we were sitting across from each other at the dinner table, celebrating my birthday he said to me "I find myself wanting to tell you that I love you before we part ways or end a conversation on the phone. I find myself daydreaming about you all the time when we are not together. I think I am in love with you and I want to be in a serious relationship with you." he said as he held my hand with his left hand and caressed my face with the other. He leaned in and kissed me gently on my forehead. I was always told that a kiss on the forehead reflected just how much a man truly cares about you. I was all in at this point "I feel the same way babe". He got up and walked around me where he was facing my back and he said "I have a surprise for you. Close your eyes." I closed my eyes in anticipation for what was to come, and I feel something cold drape around my neck. I reached my hands up to feel and opened my eyes simultaneously.

"Happy Birthday Alyssa, this is just the beginning."

"Oh, my goodness, thank you babe, it's beautiful" I said as I was fighting back tears.

No one had ever thought this much of me and the necklace was beautiful, it was obvious that it was not inexpensive at least to someone my age. He walked back around to his chair "You like it baby?"

"I love it, I hope you didn't spend too much on it" I said while blushing. He took my hand and kissed it softly "I would do anything to make you happy". He threw his napkin in his plate that he had cleaned "the food was delicious, now what's next on the agenda, it's your night we are going to do whatever you want". It was this night that I gave into temptation that had been building up inside of me. I shared the same feelings for him and I wanted to share all of me with him. I could not think of anything else I wanted to do but him.

"How about we just go back to my place and watch a movie." We had done this, many times before and he had never tried to cross any lines but, on this night, I was hoping that he did. We got up and walked out of the restaurant, he held on to my waist as we walked out. He opened the car door as he always did, and I reached over to make sure his door was unlocked. He drove to my apartment which was about 5 minutes from the restaurant. Kareem was such a perfect gentleman and it made me fall in love with him even more. When we got inside, I asked "Do you mind if I change into something a little more comfortable?" You know this was code for I'm bout to put something on that you won't be able to resist.

"Sure, go ahead, I will just sit on the couch and look through your movies to see what I can find."

"Okay. I'll be right back" I walked into my bedroom and I lit some candles on the dresser. I was rummaging through my drawer trying to find something that was not too obvious but would send the message that I wanted him. Then I started having second thoughts *maybe I should just wait*. I pulled out of my pink Victoria Secret shorts and a black tank top. I walked back out of the room and he didn't even look up.

"I found a couple of movies, tell me which one you wanna to

watch?" He said as he glanced back up and did a double take "wow when you said comfortable, I thought you meant some sweats like you usually do" he said with a smirk. I tried to play it off "Yeah it was kind of warm and I was getting a headache."

"Oh no ma'am we can't have that on your birthday. Sit down let me rub your shoulders for you."

"Okay, how about we play a little soft music and just talk for a while. We can watch the movie in a few." I shuffled through my CD catalog and found the one labeled 'grown and sexy' and slipped it in the CD player. I sat down next to him and we started conversing about what our expectations were in a relationship. He started rubbing my shoulders "ooouu babe you are so tense, no wonder you are feeling that headache coming on. What are you stressed about? Lay down let me give you a massage, I give good massages" he said as he spread his hands and cracked his fingers.

"I love a good massage but don't get any ideas" I said it, but I didn't mean it. I smiled innocently and then laid face down on the couch.

"Now if I'm going to do this I have to do it right. How about you we do this in the room on the bed and get me some baby oil or lotion" he said as he gently pulled me off the couch. I looked at him suspiciously. "Don't worry, I'm not going to try anything unless you want me to". He laughed, and I smirked. "Have you ever been to a massage therapist and had a massage?"

"No."

"Well I'm going to give you the full experience." We walked to the bedroom and pulled out the baby oil and the lotion "which one do you want?"

"I'll take the baby oil." The music was softly playing the lights were out, but the candles were lit creating a romantic ambience. I crawled up on the bed and laid down on my stomach. He gently pushed my tank top up but was struggling a bit since I was laying on the front of it. "Can you take this off and your bra too? I don't want to mess anything up?" I complied with his request. I was willing to go in whatever direction he took this, and I am sure that he knew it. He started at my shoulders, rubbing them ever so gently. His hands were warm and strong, and they felt good against my skin. Those warm and fuzzy feeling soon emerged only this time the intensity was overwhelming. I could feel my body relaxing as though I was releasing every burden I had ever carried in my life. I was like putty in his hands and he had the ability to create a masterpiece. He put some baby oil in his hands and rubbed them together. As his hands drifted down to the middle of back, I could feel chills down my spine.

"Your skin is so soft" he said.

"Thank you" I whispered just loud enough for him to hear me. His strong hands were moving down to my lower back as he massaged in a circular motion. By this time, I was feeling the warmth in between my thighs. He took one finger and gently ran it from the top of my spine to the small of my back. I was squirming a bit because it was like a fire had been lit on the inside. The tingly feeling had moved in between my legs and the flood gates had been broken. He gently kissed me on the small of my back and I moaned softly and exhaled deeply. "How was that?" he asked.

"Amazing" I said as I turned over and faced him. Of course, my breast was now fully exposed, and the high beams were on. He turned his head to look away and he tried to stand up. It was clear that he was still trying to be a gentleman and show his respect for me.

That only made me want him even more. I grabbed his arm. "Wait where are you going?"

"I just don't want you to do anything that you are not ready for. I don't want you to think that I am trying to take advantage of you either."

"I know, but I want to do this. I want you to be my first and I don't want to wait any longer."

He looked me deep in my eyes and professed his love for me. "Alyssa, you know I love and respect you, I want this to work between us. Are you sure?"

"I'm sure Kareem" I said as I became lost in his gaze. We both leaned in, our lips met, and we kissed each other passionately. I didn't really know what I was doing, it was my first time, so I let him take the lead. He undressed me from head to toe and he explored every inch of my body and I made no effort to stop him. It was as if his tongue was a paintbrush and I was his canvas. He awakened spots that I never even knew existed that caused me to reach new heights. He placed his hands in between my thigh and began to gently massage my sweet spot. My moaning got louder and louder. It was as if the louder I got the more it turned him on. Our bodies pressed together and became intertwined. I could feel his manhood entering slowly. He took his time with me and with every thrust to go in deeper, I gripped the sheets. I turned my head toward the pillow and bit down. Every stroke sent me to a place that I could not describe. He was in deep and I could feel him at every angle. I was hooked. I had never experienced these types of feelings with anyone else and I didn't want to. I climaxed first although I did not know what was happening. It felt as though I had lost control of my body, my heart was racing, my toes clenched, and the sheets were ruined. Once he climaxed we just laid there trying to catch our breath, a smile crossed both of our faces.

His body straddled over me as he continued to kiss me all over my body as if he simply could not get enough of me. He turned me over and kissed from the top of my neck to the small of my spine and it sent chills through my entire body. As he came back up and he stopped at my neck, he whispered in my ear "I love you and I am never letting you go". The way those words rolled off his tongue ignited a fire inside of me. *I am in love with this man*, I thought to myself. He was my first everything....my first love.... the first man I kissed...the first man that I had sex with. I just knew that he would be my forever.

APOLOGIES

Months went by and we became inseparable, we were together every moment that we were not working or in class. As time went on, I learned some new tricks and he was my instructor. I was so in love with this man, I did everything for him and he did everything for me and the sex --- mind blowing. I don't know if this is because I had never experienced anything else, but I knew that this was a feeling I wanted to feel forever. Things became so intense between the two of us that I ended up giving him a key to my place. It seemed that he was there all the time anyway or we were out together, *why not?* He started working at a club on the weekends doing security and when he got off he would come by my apartment. I did not always like to be waken up with the phone calls of him saying that he was on his way, but I loved waking up with him next to me. I could just melt into his strong, muscular arms. He made me feel so secure and protected.

One day he asked me to come out to the club that he was working at and just hang out, so we could go home together. I did not have anything going on that night, so I happily obliged. I had stopped going to clubs as much when we became official because I didn't want that to be a conflict so when he asked me to go I was thrilled to go out and hang out with some friends. I met my friend Stacy there and we had a blast. Anytime a man approached me either Kareem or one of the other security was there to intervene.

Apparently, he had all the security there watching me, and he was always somewhere lurking as well.

At the end of the night, as we were leaving I heard a huge commotion outside of the club. I see Kareem in the center of this commotion arguing with another man. I could hear this man say to Kareem "You and your bitch can get the fuck out of my house". Suddenly, a look of bewilderment fell over my face. *Who on earth was he talking about and what was going on?*

I had never even been to his house as odd as that seems. We were always with one another and I never questioned why he had never invited me to his house. I knew that he stayed with a group of guys who shared a bachelor pad and just figured that he did not want me around a lot of men. He was possessive in that sense, he never wanted me around his guy friends or any other man that I was not related to for that matter.

I knew what I heard though and it was not sitting well with me. I approached him and told him to calm down and walk away from the situation. Kareem had a sort of crazed look on his face like a wild animal stalking its prey. It was almost as if I could feel the heat radiating from his body like a fire had been lit within him. The man then said, "Yeah you better let your other bitch get you". Before I could process exactly what he said, Kareem charged at this man and a fight had ensued. The chaos at that moment was more than I had expected. Quite frankly, I was wondering why his roommate was now referring to me as his "other bitch". My heart dropped, and I was in disbelief and clueless as to what was this was about and why he was really keeping me from his house? Once the fight had been broken up and the confusion had died down we left to go back to my place. The entire ride home was quiet, you could hear a pin drop, neither of us said a word. The silence was eerie. I could not seem to gather my thoughts. Once we entered the house I said to him "what was that man talking about Kareem, why did he refer to me as your other *bitch*? Hell, why did he refer to me as a bitch at all? Do they know that I am your woman?"

"He was just trying to start some mess between you and me."

"Why would he want to do that? Who is this other bitch that he is referring to?"

"Alyssa, I swear to you it is nothing."

My mind was swirling with questions and the next thing I wanted to know was why I have never been to his house after dating for almost a year and being serious for about 9 months out of that year. At this point I became livid because after all this time I had never been suspicious of anything and now suddenly I was overly suspicious. I was questioning everything.

"You have a key to my house and open access, why have I never been to your house?" I said firmly.

"Alyssa, we have always just gone out or I come over here. There is always a ton of guys at my house just hanging out, I didn't want you over there for one of them to hit on you and I lose my cool. I know how my temper is. Listen, if you just give me some time to let all this cool down with my roommate and get something in place so that when you come by, you won't have to deal with a whole crowd of men then I will make sure that you can come to my place too. Just trust me."

He seemed so sincere and I wanted to believe him. I trusted him, so I said "okay, but you know I am not the type of woman that will put up with no foolishness." We continued on with our usual arrangements. We continued to spend all our free time together and I thought *there is no way that he has any time to have anything else going on* therefore I took him at this word. Trust is the foundation of any good relationship. I needed to trust and believe that he would take care of my heart the way that I took care of his and I did so blindly.

I had started going to the club regularly every weekend because he wanted me to be there. Besides that, it gave me an opportunity to pay more attention to what was going on with him and other women that he encountered at the club on a regular basis. Kareem said it was just another opportunity for him to see me and spend a little time with me since he worked so much. He had two jobs and his time was very limited. I worked fulltime and went to school fulltime, so my time was limited as well. We had to make due the best way we could. A couple of weeks after the incident happened we deviated from our original arrangement of him coming back to my place after leaving work. On this night he came to me as the club was closing and he handed me the key to his place, along with a piece of paper with directions to get there from the club. He said "meet me back at my house, here is your key, my bedroom is the last door on the left but if you don't feel comfortable going to the back of the house without me you can wait for me upfront in the living room. There shouldn't be anybody there. My roommates are out of town this weekend. I'll be right behind you, just give me about 20 minutes to finish up here" and he held my face and kissed me on my forehead. I was too happy to respond with words, the only response I could give him was a smile. I was glowing, at that moment all my doubts and suspicions were erased. I felt crazy for questioning his motives.

He obviously would not have given me a key and open access to his house if he had anything to hide or another woman living there. I arrived at the house and of course, being the woman that I am, I wanted to look around to dispel any ideas that a woman had been there. I walked to the back and entered the last room on the left. There he had a picture of he and I on his nightstand beside his bed which confirmed that this was his room. I took a deep breath and breathed a sigh of relief. I was in this far too deep to find out something of that magnitude had gone wrong. I stretched out on his bed. He had this blue suede material blanket on his bed. It felt like velvet against my skin. I sat up and looked around at how the room was put together. The walls were bare, no decorations anywhere, his shoes were sprawled out on the floor; it was a typical bachelor pad. The place could use a woman's touch, but I wasn't going to force that on him. Kareem walked in the door just as he said he would about 20 min later. I could hear his footsteps heading towards the bedroom where I was. He walked in and sat on the bed beside me "I told you I was gonna get this straight" he said.

I wrapped my arms around his around his neck and confessed "I never had any doubts". I was lying through my teeth, but I wanted him to know that I trusted him. We embraced one another, and he turned to me and asked, "Do you want to take a shower?" He knew that was my usual routine when we came home from the club. I would walk straight to the bathroom and turn the shower on. I couldn't stand the stench of the cigarette smoke that seems to get absorbed into my skin or the fact that the club would be so hot and humid that my skin would feel sticky.

"Babe, I don't have any clothes here or any of the things I need to shower".

"I took the liberty of picking you up a few things for tonight from your place earlier, I stopped by the store and bought you a toothbrush and a few other things I know you use, it is in the bathroom and you have access to anything else in the bathroom". He opened his top drawer and showed me the clothes that he bought from my house. *How could I say no.* "Wow babe, you did all that for me? Thanks love" I gently pecked him on the lips "I'm going to take a shower now." I walked into the bathroom which was located across the hall from his bedroom and I saw a grocery bag on the counter. "Babe is this the bag of stuff you bought me on the counter?" I yelled out.

"Yea"

I opened the bag to find a pink shower pouf, Oil of Olay body wash, a pink shower cap, a pack of razors, and a pink toothbrush." Kareem knew that pink was my favorite color. *So thoughtful.* I turned the water on and adjusted the knobs to get the water just the right temperature. I loved the water hot but not too hot that it would melt my skin off. I undressed and stepped into the shower. The water was hot just like I liked it and the steam was filling the bathroom and fogging the mirrors. Kareem walked into the bathroom and pulled back the shower curtain "Do you mind if I join you?" Kareem was standing there naked bearing it all. Kareem had a body that any women would vie for. He had a very chiseled physique with cuts in all the right places. He had a tattoo of praying hands on the left side of his chest and an eagle that spread its wings across his shoulder blades on his back. I looked him up and down, from head to toe and I knew that this was going to be a good night. "Of course, you can join me" I answered as I bit my bottom lip. He stepped into the shower, grabbed the soap and lathered the soap on my back. He kissed me on my neck and pressed his body against mine. He caressed my body starting at my waist and his hands just glided up to my breasts. I could feel his excitement from behind as the water and suds ran down my back. He turned me around and we began to kiss with such passion, the feelings were intense and difficult to contain. He placed his hands around my hips and picked me up and I wrapped my legs around his waist. I could feel him push his love inside and my entire body became weak. He held me up against the shower wall and the water continued to trickle down over our bodies. He held me with such ease and I grabbed on and held on tight for the ride he was about to take me on. He held on to me as he stepped out of the shower, still inside me and walked across the hall to the bed. He laid me down never losing his place in the warmth that was in between my legs. "whose is this?" he whispered in my ear. I could feel my body nearing the climax "it's ----all ----yours baby" I yelled out in between moans. I had to brace myself to keep head from hitting the back of the headboard.

"Damn right" he muttered under the loud clapping noise along with the head board beating against the wall. Between my moaning and screaming, the steady and rhythmic beating on the wall and clapping noise you would have thought we had a live band playing in the room. The way he made me feel mind, body and soul, kept me in a state of eternal flight. He was right, I was all his, there was no way anybody else could come close to the way he made me feel and I wasn't interested in looking.

Things between us continued to progress beautifully. We had connected on a whole new level and our relationship had become very serious to the point that we were now discussing marriage. It had been about 3 months since we had started switching up our routine and coming to his house more. It was kind of awkward coming to his house while his roommates were there. I did not like to be around them especially the one that called me out my name and started that confusion between us that night.

We decided that it was better for us to move in together before actually tying the knot and so we began looking for places together. I know that it was not ideal in terms of spirituality, but we were already practically living together in sin. We found the perfect spot and we were full of excitement when we were approved to move in and signed our new lease--together. It was a nice three-bedroom home in a quiet neighborhood, a perfect starter home for us. We were scheduled to move in 30 days after we signed the lease. This gave me time to put in notice at the apartment complex I was staying in and

Kareem time to give his roommates some notice. To my surprise, things were about to take a strange turn and I was not ready for it.

HERE WE GO AGAIN

We were lying in bed one morning at his house. It was early, the birds were chirping, and the sun had barely peeked through the clouds. I laid there cuddled in Kareem's arms with my head on his chest. I was awake, but my eyes were closed, and I was trying to muster up the energy to roll out of bed. Suddenly, I hear a loud banging on the front door. Startled by the noise, I jumped up and Kareem did too. He grabbed his shorts that were lying beside the bed and pulled them up around his waist. He walked over to window and peeked through the blinds of the window "Oh my God" he said under his breath. He turned and looked at me with a fearful look in his eyes as if he had seen a ghost and suddenly my heart sank. I did not know what was going on, but I got an uneasy feeling that the shit was about to hit the fan. At that moment, I hear a woman screaming "open the door Kareem" and banging as hard as she could on the front door. She then came around to his window and began to bang on the window "Open the door, Kareem! Who do you have in there this time?"

My face turned to stone, I was in shock and infuriated at the same time. *This time?* I thought. I got up to go and answer the door, but Kareem grabbed me and begged me not to.

"Shhhhhh….shhhhh…. I'll explain everything just please do not go to the door" Kareem pleaded in a whispering tone. "Just let her leave" he whispered.

A feeling of doubt settled in all over my body. It was as if I was falling down a never-ending pit and I couldn't grab a hold of anything to break my fall. *What was he hiding and how long had he been hiding it for?* I was in such shock that I could not speak. I could not argue or shout. I just wanted some answers. I peeked out the window as I heard the woman walking back to her car. The first thing I noticed was her car and I thought *I have seen that car before.* Then she got in the car, I caught a glimpse of her face and I thought, *I know this woman.* I went to high school with her. Her name is Sadie Carpenter we were not exactly friends in high school, but we were cordial. *What was going on here, why was she at his doorstep banging on the door and screaming at the top of her lungs?* I needed answers and with everything that we had pending I needed them now.

Kareem sat on the edge of the bed shaking his head. He placed his hand over his face and said "there is something that I have to tell you. This isn't easy for me to----"

"You're damn right you have something to tell me and you better start talking fast" I responded angrily with my arms folded before he could finish his sentence. Probably in that moment, I had turned into the neck rolling, eye rolling female that is often characterized as 'ghetto' or 'rachet' but I could have cared less.

"Ok look, there is no easy way to say this…. That woman that was at the door is my ex- girlfriend."

"Okay, so what reason does your ex have to come here?"

"She told me a couple of months ago that she was pregnant with my child." Kareem said fearful of my reaction.

"What? How on earth would she think that she is pregnant with your child? We have been dating for over a year. There is no way that she could think that she is pregnant by you unless... you have been chea----"

I stood up and gathered my things there was no way he could explain his way out of this. The tears were flowing, I was an emotional wreck. These tears were fueled by anger, disappointment, sadness and regret.

He grabbed my arm as I was about to walk out the front door "Alyssa listen, I made a mistake, but you have to believe me, it was an accident."

"An accident? You selfish asshole! You let me make a fool of myself...I trusted you!" I shouted as I pushed his hand off my arm.

"Alyssa wait, it was about six months ago, and she came by to get some things that she left over here. I had been drinking and one thing lead to another. Ughh... I'm so sorry Alyssa, I never meant for you to find out like this and I was going to tell you, but I wanted to find out if the baby was really mine. Alyssa...Please! Don't leave like this. I was wrong, I made a mistake but please let me make it up to you." He sobbed. This dude literally had tears coming out his eyes.

"How da hell do you think that you can make this up to me? Huh? Are you serious right now?" I was distraught because my heart was broken. The man that I had entrusted with my heart had violated my trust. We were scheduled to move into our new place together in a few weeks. We had already signed a lease that I was sure we could not get out of.

"Alyssa, please forgive me! I love you! I fucked up but I'm sorry."

"You're sorry alright. I'm done Kareem, you made your bed now lay in it wit yo baby momma" I said as I slammed the door and got in my car. I could not stop the tears from gushing. It felt as though my whole world just stopped as though I was frozen in time. It felt like my heart had been ripped out of my chest and I was barely clinging to life.

I turned the radio off in my car and rode home in complete silence. I didn't want to chance a song coming on the radio that would spark any good memories with Kareem and the odds were high that it would. I sat at the stop light with a face full of tears. The woman in the car beside me looked in at me and quickly looked away. I finally pulled up at my apartment and I gathered my things out of the car and walked through the door. It seemed that every direction I looked in there was something there to remind me of him. I fell to my knees bawling thinking to myself, *how could he do this to me? Why?* In the blink of an eye the picture-perfect relationship that we had built together was gone. I tried to gain my composure and I walked to my bedroom and laid down. I cried so hard, I had given myself a headache. I decided to take a Tylenol and take a nap to relieve the stress that I was feeling at that moment.

EXPECTING

I walked around those next couple of weeks feeling depressed. I didn't know how to deal with the fact that I had to move into this new house alone and deal with the added expenses alone. He called my phone and came by my apartment every chance that he got, and I left all his calls unanswered and text messages unread. He sent me flowers and left cards and candy on my doorstep only for me to toss them in the trash when I walked in the door. I had the apartment company change the locks on my doors because I didn't want to find him in my apartment when I came home. I just wanted him out of my life. He had done enough damage. I began feeling sick, and I had missed my cycle. I just assumed that it was from the stress of everything that had happened. I decided to go and get checked out considering he had admittedly cheated on me, I wanted to get a thorough exam anyway. I made an appointment for the following day at my doctor's office.

I walked into the doctor's office, my stomach in knots, the anxiety alone was more than I could bear. I had no idea what to expect but I was hoping that I would learn that stress was causing my illness. I had been nauseous, dizzy, and fatigued.

"Alyssa Calloway" the nurse called out. I got up and walked to the back. "What are you being seen for?" the nurse asked.

"I have been sick lately, nauseous and fatigued. My cycle is a couple weeks late, but I think it is because I have been stressed out lately."

"Oh no, what have you been stressed out about?" she asked.

"I just recently found out that my boyfriend cheated on me, with that being said, I would like to be checked for everything."

"No problem Miss Calloway let me go and grab a few things and I will be right back in the meantime would you mind giving me a urine specimen?" I was looking for a reaction, but she did not have one. I guess she probably hears of cases such as this all the time in this line of work.

I went into the bathroom and provided them with the urine specimen and as I walked out of the bathroom the nurse was standing there with a bunch of tubes to draw blood. She also swabbed my mouth to perform an HIV screening. Once the nurse had finished collecting what she needed, she escorted me back to the back in the examination area. I waited there for the doctor to come in and every second seemed like an hour. About 20 minutes passed and the doctor walked in "Good afternoon, Miss Calloway"

"Hello how are you Dr. Lawson"

"I am well Miss Calloway, what can I do for you today?"

"Well doc, I just want to be tested for everything. I just found out that my boyfriend cheated on me and to be on the safe side, I would like to be tested for everything." I said nervously.

"Okay, I understand. Wise decision. I am going to step out of the room for a few minutes. I would like for you to undress from the waist down and I will be back to run some more tests."

He stepped out for a few minutes while I undressed and knocked on the door to come back in.

"Come in."

Dr. Lawson walked in and completed his examination with me. The nurse came back in the room and gave him some lab work results. He glanced over the labs and said "well Miss Calloway, I have some good news"

I breathed a sigh of relief and said "Thank God, okay great Doc"

"He said your HIV screening came back negative, it doesn't look like there are any signs of any STD's however we will have to wait a couple of days for the labs to come back to confirm. Should anything come back abnormal we will give you a call but if you don't hear back from our office then you know everything is good to go. No news is good news. Also, congratulations are in order."

"Congratulations?" I asked. *Was he congratulating me because I was STD free?* I thought

"Yes, your pregnancy test came back positive. Based on the date of your last menstrual cycle you are about 6 weeks. That would explain the nausea and fatigue. I'm gonna prescribe you some multi-vitamins and iron supplements because your iron is low, and you certainly need to get that up. I want to see you back in 2 weeks so that we can check for a heartbeat and run some other tests to get your prenatal care going. Did you have any other questions for me?"

"Are you sure I'm pregnant Doc? We had not been trying to have a baby. I have been on birth control pills for years and I only missed a few pills recently."

"You are definitely pregnant Miss Calloway, there is no doubt about that. These things happen all the time unexpectedly. You can go ahead and get dressed and I will see you back in a couple of weeks."

I sat there on the bed trying to wrap my mind around the idea that I was pregnant especially given the circumstances. My boyfriend who was now my ex-boyfriend had just cheated on me with a woman who may also be pregnant with his child and I was just getting ready to start my senior year of college. I had been taking classes every summer since I started so that I could finish early, and it had literally knocked off a year of my four-year degree. I had also taken classes in high school that granted me college credit, so I had a head start so to speak. Here I was, 21 and pregnant. I did not want anything to hinder me from finishing something that was so important to me. If felt like a ton of brick had been released on my shoulders. *How could this be happening to me?* I thought about how disappointing this was going to be for my parents to find out. Then I thought about how this information could also impact Kareem. I had to tell him, I could not very well withhold this information. It would be unfair. I was a woman of virtue. I left the doctor's office with a million and one thoughts swirling in my mind.

It felt like a funnel cloud had dropped down in head. My thoughts were scrambled, and nothing seemed to make sense. I had so much at stake, we were scheduled to move into our home next week, but we had been broken up for almost a month and now I am pregnant with his child. Do I try to work things out with him? I was weighted by the confusion I felt but I had to face this head on after all I was going to be someone's mother soon. I decided to accept Kareem's next phone call as I knew that one would surely be coming soon. About 3 hours later, about the time that he got off work, my phone rang. I picked up the phone and looked at the caller Id and it was in fact Kareem on the other end. I took a deep breath and answered the phone "Hello".

"Alyssa, how are you? Are you okay? I miss you so much." He said with excitement.

"Hi Kareem, I'm okay, I really need to talk to you. We have some things that we need to work through. When can you meet me at my place?" I had to keep the conversation short and to the point. I had to meet him at my place because I never wanted to go back to his place again. I would be reminded of the day that my world was shattered into a million pieces and I did not want to replay that experience again.

"I can come by now if you want me to. I am leaving work and I can head over there right now."

"Okay, come on by" I said calmly. I really was not ready to see him, but I knew that this was not the type of information that I needed to withhold for any length of time and I wanted to just go ahead and put it all on the table. Unlike him!

"Okay, I am on my way to you now. Do you need me to bring you anything?"

"No thanks." I replied.

A short while later, I heard a knock at the door. I looked through the peep hole and Kareem was standing there with a bouquet of roses. I opened the door and invited him in. He handed me the roses and said, "these are for you".

I rolled my eyes and accepted the roses and laid them on the counter. I wanted to go ahead and get this conversation out of the way. It was way too difficult sitting face to face with him. All the feelings that I felt for him came flooding back and I realized how utterly in love with him I truly was despite his indiscretion.

"Listen, I have something that I need to...."

Kareem interjected and said "Wait, before you go on, please just hear me out. I never knew what love was until you came into my life. I cannot lose you. Please give me one more chance to make this right between us. I have been sick these last few weeks."

"Yeah me too." I said sarcastically. "As I was saying, I need to tell you something very important." I added.

"Okay" Kareem said hopelessly.

"I went to the doctor today to get checked, you know, since your indiscretion has left me in that position. The doctor told me that I am pregnant."

"Oh my God! That is great news Alyssa, if I am going to have a child with anyone I want it to be you".

Here he is excited about the news and I am completely distraught. "Great news? Are you kidding me? Do you realize what we are going through right now? Not to mention I haven't finished school yet. What about this other woman who could potentially be carrying your child?"

"Alyssa, I promise you that I am going to be here with you through this whole experience to make sure you complete your goals. I never really believed that the child that she is carrying is mine in the first place. That is the main reason I did not tell you about it right away and I wanted to wait to get a paternity test. If it is mine, then I will just have to do the right thing, but I am sure that it's not. The fact is that you are pregnant now, we can't change that. This is divine intervention telling us that we need to work through this for the sake of our child not to mention you and I both know that we really love each other."

"It's going to be difficult for me to trust you again, you know that right?"

"I know it will and I am willing to do whatever I have to do earn that trust back." He said convincingly.

"We are scheduled to move into our house this week do you think that we should proceed with that move or should we go and talk to the realtor to see if we can get out of that?" I already knew how he would answer the question, but I asked anyway.

"I think we should just go forward with our plans, we need to have a place for the baby when he or she gets here. Right?"

I had some tough decisions to make and not a lot of time. I was young, just barely 21 years old and even though I was mature for my age, it didn't change the fact that I was young and expecting a child. Many of my peers had already had children, some had children right out of high school and some were pregnant when we graduated. I knew many of them were struggling and that was not the lifestyle that I wanted to bring my child into. I had a whole plan for my life, I would finish college, get settled into my career, get married and then have kids. By my calculations, I was several years ahead of where I wanted to be, and I was missing a marriage certificate and an established career.

One thing I knew for sure, I did not want to raise my child in a single parent home. I have heard the horror stories and it scared me to death. I knew that I needed to do everything in my power to afford my child the opportunity to grow up with both parents. So...I decided to take Kareem back. After all, he seemed so sincere in his apology and we all make mistakes, right? All the red flags were there. I simply chose to abate them all with a couple of elements to hold us together, hope and a baby.

BLINDSIDED

We went forward with our plans to move in. He would not allow me to touch a thing, he just wanted me to take it easy and relax throughout the moving process. He didn't want me to do anything to risk me losing the baby. Things were beginning to look up although we had a long road ahead of us. We had constant contact when he was at work and he had been very attentive to my needs. Our sex life on the other hand was non-existent. I would not let him touch me. I was doing good just to be in the same space with him. I was working through the trust issues and I was sick as a dog most days which didn't help. As the weeks passed, I grew more and more ill to the point that I was taking a lot of time off work and school.

One night when Kareem was working late, I got a craving for some ice cream, so I headed out to pick up a pint of Ben and Jerry's cookie dough ice cream from the grocery store. When I pulled up I notice that there was a car in the front that resembled Sadie Carpenter's car. She had a very distinct car, an electric blue older model Camaro. I walked into the grocery store and she was there standing in line. I studied her, and I noticed that this woman did not look pregnant at all let alone 7 or 8 months pregnant. I stood there looking baffled, *how could this be?* Either she had lied to him or he had not been completely honest with me and given his current track record I was inclined to go with the latter. I approached her as she reached the door.

"Heyyyyy Sadie, do you remember me? She looked me up and down for a moment.

"Oh yeah, Alyssa, right?"

"Yes, that's right, how have you been?"

"I've been good, what about you?"

"I can't complain" I was trying to think of a way to ask her about Kareem, but I did not want to seem obvious. At this point what did I have to lose.

"Hey, listen, do you know a guy named Kareem?"

She rolled her eyes and then looked at me with concern "Yeah I know Kareem, he is my ex-boyfriend. We just separated about 3 months ago. Why do you ask?"

"Did you say 3 months ago?" I suddenly felt the wall crumbling around me, but I had to remain strong. I did not want her to see me show any signs of weakness.

"Why do you ask, did you hear that we were supposed to get married soon or something?"

"Married?" I had a big lump in my throat.

"Yeah girl, we were supposed to get married. We were living together up until about 6 months ago. We were having some problems and we were arguing all the time and I decided that rather than being up under his roommates, that I would get a place that we could move to. I found us a place and he was supposed to move in with me but a couple months later he started getting distant. Girl, one day I heard that he was at the house with another woman, so I went by there and I was standing out there…."

I interjected "banging on the door, right?

"Yea, chile when I found out he was seeing someone else I dropped him like a bad habit and I haven't looked back."

"Girl it's a good thing you didn't get pregnant by him or anything?" I said rubbing my belly, trying to play it cool. "That would have made things a little trickier."

"Pregnant, girl please?" she snickered. "Honey I don't have any kids and I have never been pregnant and I was certainly not crazy enough to get pregnant by him. Wait, where is all of this coming from?" She said very in a very matter of fact tone. She made me feel like I was crazy because here I was pregnant by him.

"I was the woman in that house that day, but I knew nothing about any other woman. To my knowledge, we were exclusive and in a serious relationship. I had a key to his house and he had keys to mine. He told me that you thought that you were pregnant and that there was a possibility that he had fathered the child. We broke up for a little while because for you to be six months pregnant he would have had to have cheated on me, but we ended up getting back together." I said hesitantly.

"Alyssa, classmate to classmate, if I were you, I would run as fast as I could away from that man. He is a pathological liar and a whore. He cheated on me with not just you and he will do it again. You know the old saying once a dog always a dog." She clutched her bag and walked right on out of the store.

I didn't know how to process that information. Was she telling me this as a bitter ex who just wanted to sabotage his current relationship. It is possible that she had lied to him about being pregnant and that he really thought that she was. I was floored by this overwhelming conversation with her. *Why was she open to share these details?* This was a conversation that I was going to have to keep to myself and just pay attention to the things going on around me.

Her words replayed in my mind like a broken record. Could the man that I am having a child with be a player? If he was, he was very good at it because I wondered how on earth he could find time to carry on two committed relationships. *What am I going to do? How will I address this? Should I address this?* She could be lying too, there was no real way to tell. He had already told me of his indiscretion and perhaps it was just that and she knew that he was dealing with me, so she wanted to say something to ruin our relationship. I was certainly driving myself crazy trying to find the answers to these questions.

About a week had passed since my run in with Sadie. I continued to keep it to myself and just pay attention to his whereabouts and his actions. For all practical purposes, I was intentionally ignoring all the red flags to keep my family together. Things had been decent between us although I had been somewhat distant from him. He continued to make every effort to get closer to me. This situation with Sadie was not making it any easier to let my guard down again. I decided that it was time to ask about Sadie and find out if he had any contact with her just to see how this conversation went. You know, I wanted to fill him out a bit. When he came in from work that night I had dinner prepared. The smell of savory home cooked food filled the air. "oouuu, it smells good in here. What did you cook?"

"I made your favorite, smothered pork chops, rice and gravy and broccoli covered with cheese."

"Yes!!!" he shouted. "I'm starving.". We sat down at the table to eat.

We engaged in some small talk and then I hit him with the big question. "So, isn't it about time for your ex to be giving birth pretty soon?" I said as I was pushing my food around on the plate.

"I do not know when she is due. I haven't talked to her since that day that she came to the house. Knowing how she is, I'm sure that once she has the baby she will be in touch and we can go through with the DNA test at that time. Until then, I am not worried about her, I am worried about you and the child that you are carrying. I know this one mine". He said as he rubbed my belly.

"Are you sure it was just a one-time thing that you had with her while we were together. You really need to be completely honest with me."

"Yes, it only happened once, I swear". He said with his left hand up and his right hand on his chest. "Now I don't want you worrying your pretty little head about that, you hear me? You know I don't like you stressin bout anything. It's not good for the baby." He leaned over and kissed me on my forehead. I smiled and excused myself from the table.

A couple of days later I went to work with everything still heavy on my mind. I had been sick most of the day, but I managed to make in into work and complete my day. I worked in a retail store in the mall and it was time for us to close. As I was pulling down the gate I was approached by a woman who was the girlfriend of one of the other security guards at the club where Kareem worked, her name was Tianna. "Hey girl" she said.

"Hey Tianna."

"I haven't seen you at the club lately, why haven't you been out there?"

I had not shared with anyone but Kareem that I was pregnant, and I wanted to keep it under wraps until I was well into my second trimester. I was close but not quite there yet. My pregnancy and the drama that we had recently gone through was of course the real reason that I had not been out there, but I would not dare share that with her. "Kareem and I just moved into our new place. I have been so busy with that lately."

"Oh, ok well girl, you may want to come back out there and check on Kareem, chile".

"Whatchu mean check on him? For what?"

"I don't want to be the bearer of bad news, but I like you. I think you are a good woman, too good of a woman for the likes of his ass."

"Wait! What?" I said with a confused look on my face. My lip curled, and one eye brow raised. *Why is this woman telling me that I am* *too good for Kareem? What did she **know** that I clearly did not.*

"Girl call me when you leave here. There are some things that you need ta know about Kareem specially since y'all livin together now". She handed me a piece of paper with her number on it and I accepted and shoved it down into my pocket. I knew that my heart could not take much more, and I could not believe that another person was coming to me with a warning about him. I could not wait until I clocked out to find out what she had to say. It was not like she had anything to gain by telling a lie on Kareem, so it was worth listening too. As soon as I hit the door to walk to the car I started dialing her number. The phone rang, and she answered "Hello".

"Hey this is Alyssa. I was calling you back to hear what you had to tell me about Kareem".

"Hey girl. Chile, I hate to tell you this, I'm just gonna come right out and say it, Kareem is cheating on you. I have known for a long time, but I have not said anything because of my man. He woulda' had a fit if I woulda' said something about his friend and got him in some trouble but after getting to know you some I didn't feel that it was right to keep it from you any longer. I had been debating for a while but honestly, I thought that the way he goes through women it wouldn't last long and you would move on to someone more deserving. When I heard that you were moving in with him, I was like oh hell nah, that ain't right she needs to know. I'm telling you this cause I think you need to know but if my man found out he would kill me so please don't tell him that I told you. I know that's your man and all, but he be doing some crazy stuff in that club, you know how ratchet some of these girls are. They don't even care that he has a woman."

My face was stone as I sat on the other end of the phone

listening to the second person tell me that my man, the father of the child that I was carrying was a scumbag. All I could think was *how in the world could this have happened to me.* I knew deep down that all these people were not just coming to me with the same version unwarranted. There was indeed some truth to what they were saying. I could not think straight the tears were pouring as I sat in my car and listened to this. I somehow felt trapped, not just in the fact that I was carrying his child but the fact that I had fallen in love with this man and my loyalty would not allow me to just give up on him just like that. As much as I knew that there was some truth to some of these accusations, I needed some receipts not just someone's word.

"I won't say anything to him about what you have told me. Honestly, I have been getting quite a few stories lately and I have just been trying to determine what's truth and what's lies. Can you tell me if there is any way that I could find out on my own, you know catch him in the act?" I was the type of person that needed physical evidence before making a decision that could alter the course of my life and most importantly the life of my unborn child.

"I wish I could tell you how to catch him in the act. He's good, I'll tell you that. You have to do what you feel is right, all I am telling you to do is pay very close attention and be careful."

"Thank you for letting me know."

I ended the call with my feelings crushed. I went home and laid in the bed and I could not stop sobbing. The tears would not stop flowing. I knew that I need to gain my composure before Kareem got home. I could not let him know that I suspected anything if I chose to attempt to catch him in the act. I had to do something to occupy my mind, so I got up and began to unload some boxes that we had still in the garage that we had yet to unpack. I lifted the boxes and brought them in the house, they were much heavier than I thought they'd be. I was no stranger to heavy lifting before I found out I was pregnant. I began to get a little winded, so I took a break. I suddenly felt a pain in my stomach, it was enough to sit me down. I laid down on the bed and I knew that Kareem would be home soon. I fell asleep and I awoke when I heard the door open. When I lifted my head, I knew something was wrong. My stomach was cramping, and I felt something trickle down my leg. I jumped up and rushed to the bathroom and what I saw broke my heart. I just knew that I was losing the child that I was carrying. "Oh my God, Kareem we have to go to the emergency room, I'm bleeding." He ran toward the bathroom "what's wrong?"

I'm bleeding and I'm in pain. This isn't supposed to be happening."

He picked me up and cradled me in his arms and raced me to the car. He was speechless. I just remember seeing this stressed look on his face, but he never uttered a word. The pain was becoming intense and I was doubled over in the seat of the car silently praying that I would not lose my baby. It was not too long ago that I had heard their first heart beat and saw the first ultra sound of the beginning stages of growth. Once we arrived at the hospital Kareem picked me up out of the car, cradling me in his arms. I laid my head on his shoulder and wrapped my hands around his neck. He got to the front desk and the receptionist said, "how can I help you sir?"

"My girlfriend is 11 weeks pregnant and she's bleeding and in a lot of pain."

"Okay sir let's get her to the back."

They immediately took me to the back and set me up in a bed. They pulled in a machine to do an ultrasound and brought in an instrument to listen for the baby's heartbeat. The nurse placed the instrument against my stomach tracing it all around my belly, but we did not hear a heartbeat. The silence was deafening.

"What is going on, is the baby okay?" Kareem shouted as he held tightly onto my hand. He was holding on so tight I was beginning to lose feeling in my hand.

"I'm sorry, it is not looking good, we cannot detect a heartbeat." Kareem clinched my hand even tighter. I was in so much pain. "Let me do an ultrasound to see if I can get a better picture." the doctor said as he squirted this cold blue gel on my stomach. He ran the instrument across my stomach and we both stared silently at the screen hoping for some good news. Kareem continued to hold my hand and squeeze tightly. "I'm sorry to tell you this but it looks like the fetus has been partially expelled we will have to perform and emergency procedure to remove what is remaining, to prevent a very serious infection."

Kareem looked at the doctor and shook his head. He released his grip on my hand and placed his hand on my stomach. I was in tears from both the emotional pain of losing my baby and the physical pain of miscarrying. I was hoping that this was just a bad dream that I would soon wake up from.

"I'm sorry sir but we have got to get her to the back, the nurse will be in to give her something for pain and she will probably be out until after the procedure has been completed." Kareem never uttered a word, but the tears that he shed spoke volumes. The nurse came in and poked around my arm trying to put in an IV. She inserted a needle into the IV "what's that?" I asked

"This is something to help you with the pain and something to keep you calm. We are going to wheel you to the back to the OR in just a few minutes. Don't worry, the doctor is going to take good care of you. You are in good hands."

"How long will she be back?" Kareem asked as he wiped away a single tear that was rolling down his cheek.

"We will keep you updated sir." She replied as she prepared the bed to move me down to the operating room.

"Alyssa, we are going to get through this together" Kareem said as he kissed my hand and then he leaned in and kissed my forehead and then my hand. I laid there in the bed in pain both physical and mental, but I could not respond. I felt numb for that moment. A different nurse came in and injected some medication into my arm and I immediately fell asleep. I awoke some hours later in the recovery room feeling groggy and disoriented. It was almost as though I was waking up from a bad dream only sadly, it was reality. I was no longer pregnant. The thought of that cut me deeply. Although I had gotten pregnant unexpectedly and in not so desirable circumstances, I had grown rather attached to the little life that was growing inside of my womb. In the blink of an eye that little life was gone. I was not sure how I would recover from this but the last thing on my mind was all the drama that I had learned about prior to me ending up here. For all I know, that drama is the reason why my unborn child never made it into this world. The stress that I carried from that could have been more than he or she could bear. I was upset, and I had no idea what to do about it. I wanted to forget about that entire night if it was possible. The nurse came in and rolled me down the hall to my room where Kareem was waiting.

"Baby how are you feeling?" he said as he caressed my face.

"I'm okay, I just want to go home"

"I am going to get her paperwork ready for the discharge as well as her discharge instructions, so you can head home and rest. The doctor will be in a moment to speak with you." said the nurse.

BREAK UP TO MAKE UP

We arrived home and I immediately went to lay down in the bed. Of course, that was part of my discharge instructions. In the days following my release I grew increasingly more depressed. Kareem would attempt to be affectionate with me and I would push him away. I withdrew from family and friends and it got to the point where I decided to take a semester off school. I took off work using my short-term disability to give myself to time to recover. I could not concentrate on anything. As a result, I took a hit on my pay and it put some pressure on Kareem, but I figured he would be understanding considering the circumstances.

As the days and weeks passed, I noticed a change in Kareem. He went from being supportive, sweet and affectionate to agitated, caustic, and distant. I didn't know if it was because I had been pushing him away or if it was the increase in responsibilities with the household bills. I knew that Kareem had a temper, but he had never in the almost two and a half years that I had known him, directed it towards me. For the first time, I faced his wrath and I was stunned.

One night he came in after work and he sat down on the edge of the bed. He seemed upset about something and I suspected that it was something that happened at work. I kneeled behind him and placed my hands on his shoulders and began to massage. I knew that I had been distant. I wanted to let him know that I was still here for him "Is everything okay baby?"

He swiped my hands away from shoulders and moved off the bed. He went straight to the shower without saying a word. Not even a "hello". I decided not to bother him and just allow him to unwind. He stepped out the shower and walked into the bedroom with the towel around his waist, skin glistening. I handed him a beer and said "what's going on? Do you want to talk about it?".

He snatched the beer from my hand and said, "what the hell do you care?"

I was taken aback by his tone and actions. *If anyone should be upset, it should be me. Why was he so upset with me?* I knew I had not done anything to deserve this treatment I asked him again "what is going on with you?" I walked toward him to give him a hug and he took the beer and doused it in my face.

"Leave me alone."

I stood there speechless unable to utter a single word. I was wiping the beer from my face with my hand, rubbing it away from my eyes. My eyes were burning, and my mouth was wide open from the shock. I could hear the fizzing as it ran down the sides of my head. I shuddered at the thought of his actions and I had no idea what would make him do such a thing. How could he go from "I love you" to "leave me alone" and douse my face with a drink without any remorse. The beer was dripping from my face and I knew that there was no way that I would tolerate such behavior from anyone. "Get out!" I yelled.

He grabbed my neck and said "This my house, I'm not going anywhere, you leave!" he shouted in my face and he tossed me down to the ground. I was in disbelief, I mean who was this man? I thought about leaving but where would I go? I could not tell anyone what he had done, if my family found out they would kill him, if my friends found out they would look at me like I was crazy. Once again, I felt trapped. I pulled myself up off the ground and I went to the bedroom and locked the door. I needed to process what had just happened. We did share this house and I knew there was no way I was leaving and apparently, he wasn't leaving either. I spread out on the bed sobbing uncontrollably. *What did I get myself into? I should have left a long time ago.* I eventually cried myself to sleep.

The next morning, I awoke and walked into the living room and he had already left to go to work. I decided to read a book to keep my mind occupied and think of something else. Later that evening Kareem walked in with a bouquet of roses. "Hey Alyssa" he said softly.

"Hey."

"I know you are mad at me, I don't blame you. You got every right to be. I don't know what got into me last night. I'm really sorry. Do you think you could ever forgive me? I understand if you can't and I'll leave if you want me to." he said as a tear rolled down his cheek. He seemed to be genuine in his apology but lately he has been full of apologies. There was still the matter of his alleged infidelity that I had yet to address but I knew that now was not the time. I accepted his apology with some reservations because now we are not only talking about infidelity but emotional and physical abuse. I did not want to find myself in an emotionally and physically abusive relationship but there was no denying that I was 110% in love with this man. We had already been through so much together. We are all human and we all make mistakes. There I was telling myself this once again trying to convince myself that his behavior was okay. It won't happen again.

It was downhill from there. I was finally released to go back to work. I took as many hours as I could, trying to play catch up with the bills. Instead of the abuse from Kareem, I received distance from him. He was working all the time or least that's what he said. It was hard to tell because whenever a bill came due that was his responsibility, it fell on me to pay it. As a result, I spent so much time at work myself that I rarely noticed his absence. His car broke down and it was irreparable therefore he needed a new one but neither of us could afford a car payment. We were down to sharing a car, my car, only I felt like I was the one who didn't have a car. Because of his hours at work, I would generally catch a ride and sometimes walk to work because of the proximity from my house to my job. It was a headache, but I always did what needed to be done to get by and I never complained.

We had gone from spending all our free time together to barely seeing each other at all. When we did see each other, it was usually when he came in, in the middle of the night when he would wake me up for a little quickie. He didn't wake me up with tender kisses. He woke me by moving my panties to the side and penetrating me from behind. I was getting absolutely no pleasure from these encounters. Then he would roll over and fall asleep. He would not even hold me and when I tried to lay on his chest he would roll over and turn his back to me. The sex had gone from mind-blowing to blah. There was a disconnect somewhere and I was beginning to feel like I was simply a warm body in the bed that he could come and get his rocks off when he needed to. I was miserable, but I kept myself distracted with work and school to keep from thinking about just how miserable I was.

One morning Kareem came to me and said "Hey baby, I'm gonna be off for the next couple of days. Why don't we do something together. We really haven't spent any quality time together and I think we need it."

I was feeling hopeful that he had extended this olive branch. I knew that something needed to happen. I was glad that he recognized the same thing. Our relationship had become mundane and it needed some rejuvenation. "That sounds good babe! I am scheduled to go to work today but I'm off tomorrow and if need be, I will call out on Sunday. What did you have in mind?"

"Well I thought we could head to the beach and have a little romantic getaway." He said as he grabbed my hips and pulled me close to him. "We need a lil us time." He was right, something had to change, and this was a step in the right direction. *This man really does love me* I thought to myself.

"Ok baby, I'm all for it. You know I love the beach." I said as I leaned in and kissed him on his sexy lips.

"Great, I will book us a room tonight and we can leave in the morning and come back Sunday evening. I got a little hook up out there on a nice room. What time do you have to be at work today? I'll drop you off and then I will pick you up when you get off."

"I have to be there in an hour and I close tonight so I'll be ready at 9:30."

I got ready for work and Kareem dropped me off at work. I went into work with a whole new attitude. I was overly happy in anticipation for this getaway we were about to take. The time flew by on my shift. Normally, it would drag by. At the end of my shift, I walked outside and waited with a new co-worker. I told him to be waiting for me outside in the parking lot at this time. After working a long shift at work and being on my feet all day, all I wanted to do was go home, take a shower, get in the bed and cuddle with my man. It was not safe to walk alone at that time of night. My co-worker's boyfriend was out in the parking lot waiting for her. I looked around and did not see my car or my man anywhere near. I called his phone, no answer. I called again straight to voicemail. That just usually meant that the phone was turned off. *Maybe his battery died,* I thought. My co-worker walked to her car and talked to her boyfriend through the window for a moment. She turned around and came back to stand with me on the curb. "I told my boyfriend that you were waiting on your boyfriend and we both agreed that it was not a good idea to leave you out here by yourself. It's just not safe. I will wait with you hun."

"Thank you so much, he should be here any minute." I said confidently. Who was I kidding this wouldn't be the first time he didn't show up on time. Hell, I don't know why I thought that he would follow through and do right by me this time. He often left me waiting. That high that I had been on all day was rapidly fading. I was just hoping and praying that he would show up soon, it was kind of embarrassing, you know. Thank goodness it was a beautiful clear and mild summer night. It was about 70 degrees and there was a full moon. There was not a cloud in sight, but the stars twinkled like diamonds hitting the light at just the right angle.

My co-worker and I stood outside while she smoked a cigarette and discussed our day on the sales floor. About 25 minutes later, her boyfriend called her back to the car. He was growing tired of waiting. I called Kareem again…. straight to voicemail. *What in the hell is he doing?* I thought to myself. My co-worker walked back over to me and said, "let's sit in the car and wait or we can just take you home." I did not want to leave because I did not want us to cross paths and miss one another but given the current timeline I was sure that he was not going to show. I grew furious although I did not let them know what I was thinking. I just smiled and said, "thank you so much, I don't live far from here." We got into the car and drove the 5 minutes it took to get home from work. As we pulled into the driveway, I see my car in the yard. I say to my co-worker and her boyfriend "thank you again for the ride and thank you for waiting with me. I apologize for any inconvenience."

"It's no problem love, have a good night and I will see you tomorrow. You are working tomorrow right?"

"No, I'm off tomorrow, I will see you soon."

Her boyfriend never uttered a word to me. It was like he was afraid to say anything to another woman, so he let her do all the talking. I shuffled through my purse and pulled out the keys, got out of the car and walked to the door. I turned the key and walked in to find Kareem laying on the couch sleeping with a bottle of Grey Goose on the coffee table beside him. The smell of vodka was pronounced. "I know this sorry ass dude did not leave me stranded at work to get drunk on the couch" I mumbled to myself in complete amazement.

"Kareem!!!! Get up!!!!" I shouted.

He sat up looked at me, rolled his eyes and laid back down. I kicked his foot and yelled again "Kareem!!! How dare you leave me waiting for you at work and you laying up here drunk and resting while I have been at work all day and waiting on you for almost an hour to pick me up…got me out here look'n stupid."

Kareem sat up so casually and rubbed his temples. "I'm sorry, I- ---I----I"

"You…you what?" I was sick of hearing I'm sorry. Those words rolled off his tongue more than anything else and it was nauseating.

"Time just got away from me Alyssa, I had a couple of drinks and I fell asleep"

Is he serious right now? I thought to myself. If looks could kill he would be a dead man right now, I cut my eyes in such a way that it would pierce your soul. I could not deal with his lack of concern for my safety.

"How did you get home?" he asked.

"I had to get my co-workers boyfriend to drive me home."

"Say what? Your co-workers boyfriend?" He shouted.

"Yes, both her and *her boyfriend* dropped me off because they waited with me for a while and you never showed" I said sarcastically.

"You let some dude drop you off at the house we share?" he said as if the only thing he heard was that another man brought me home. "Bitch you must have lost your mind" he ranted as he stood up and paced the floor.

"Bitch? Who da hell do you think you are talking to?" The nerve of this man, and I use the term man loosely. *What kind of man would leave his girlfriend stranded at work and then be upset that it was a couple that bought his girlfriend home?* What did he expect me to do, walk?

"You know what fuck you Alyssa, you get that dude to be with you then. Tell that dude to take your ass to the beach. That's why no one is ever going to want you, you a hoe. You be entertaining these dudes out here" he continued on his drunken rant.

All I could do was shake my head in disbelief. I knew he was drunk, but my mama always told me that a drunk mind speaks a sober heart. She also told me that when a man accusing a woman of something like this with no merit it was because he was doing it himself. *Is this truly how he felt?* He was accusing me of entertaining other men because he left me stranded at work and I got a ride from my co-worker and HER boyfriend. What type of backwards logic is this? If anyone should be upset, it should have been me, but it was something about when he said "no one is ever going to want you" that stuck with me. I felt trapped and most importantly I believed him. My self-esteem was at an all-time low and he was the reason. His words cut me like a thousand knives being swung at me in every direction, I could not escape the wounds that it caused. I was frustrated, hurt and inundated---I was broken.

Kareem stormed out the door and jumped in the car and left me standing there with tears streaming down my face. Who knows where he was going or what he was going to do and at this point I didn't care. I was just glad that I did not have to look at his face anymore tonight. Deep down, I knew that he was probably out with some other woman. It was like woman's intuition, aside from the stories that I had been told about him in confidence, my gut was telling me that he was with someone else. My heart however just would not let go of the man that he portrayed himself to be when we first started dating. As a result, I was taking an emotional beating that left the deepest wounds. The scars they left made me unrecognizable. I was living a lie. When I walked out the house I wore this beautiful smile, one that could light up any room but behind that smile was pain and despair. A woman that was begging to be loved and appreciated for all the good that I had to offer.

The next morning, I hear the door opening and I thought, here he comes with his "I'm sorry" and sure enough I was right. He comes in the bedroom door, and I pretended to still be asleep. I did not want to look in his face and be reminded of the way he acted the night before. I could hear him just standing there over me and it gave me an eerie feeling, but I just laid there with my eyes closed. He tapped my shoulder and I pretended to wake up. "Good morning Alyssa, did you sleep ok?"

I just sat up and looked him like *What the fuck do you think?* If I responded to this dumb question, it would surely start another argument and I was emotionally spent from last night. I had no energy to argue with him, so I said nothing.

"Listen Alyssa, I'm sorry about last night. I was wrong, I had been drinking and I wasn't thinking logically. You know how I get when I drink that Grey Goo—"

I cut him off "yeah, then you probably shouldn't be drinking it".

"You're right, I want to change my ways. I am not perfect. I have some things I need to work on, but I want you by my side. I cannot imagine going through this transformation without you." He grabbed my hand and continued "I want you to be my wife" .

"You want to marry a hoe?" I said mockingly.

"I know you are not a hoe. You are a good woman! I said a lot of things that I didn't mean Alyssa. You have got to believe me when I say that I love you. I know I'mma asshole at times, but you love me too and I thank you for loving me the way that you do despite of my flaws. I want us to start going to church together. I want us to pray together and work on ourselves together. I want you to be my forever"

I had never been a regular church goer but my faith in God was unshakeable. I prayed fervently, and I had my own relationship with Him. I had always wanted to find a good church to go to, but I had been disappointed by some of the things that I had seen and heard that took place in these churches. The preacher sleeping with half the congregation, the preacher passing the collection plate around 5 or 6 times to meet a goal that they had set but riding around in Cadillac Escalades while their followers were struggling and catching rides. I just felt that there were very few genuine churches that were just there to spread the word of God and therefore I maintained my own relationship with God. I had even gone to a church where the preacher had other members of his ministry to wipe his feet as if he were some type of God himself. The bible speaks against this type of thing, so I just tried to live my life right and did my own bible study.

The fact that he wanted to make changes and bring us together on not just an emotional level but on spiritual level peaked my interest. After all, I had a lot of time, energy and money invested in Kareem. I really wanted this to work out and if he wanted it as bad as I did then maybe we could turn our disaster into a beautiful love story. I couldn't just leave him or neglect him while he was reaching out of help. It simply was not my character. It seemed disloyal and I was not a disloyal person in the least. I had never loved anyone else and I could certainly stand to improve my relationship with The Lord.

"If you promise, to work on our relationship and work on your relationship with The Lord, I will consider marrying you, but I need to see some changes and fast."

"I will, I realized just how important you are to me and how poorly I have been treating you and you still have my back. I would be a fool to let you walk out of my life." He kissed me on my forehead and said "I'm sorry I hurt you, we are going to be alright. I love you."

"I love you too" I said to him as a single tear rolled down my cheek.

"Now are you ready to go to the beach, so I can make it all up to you? I already booked our room."

I was hesitant to go on this trip after the stunt he had pulled the night before. He had killed my excitement and I didn't know how to recover from it. At the same time, I didn't want to see him waste any money and after the revelations that he made about wanting to marry me and wanting to improve our relationship through God, I didn't want to say no. I tried to make the best of it. I didn't want to be the reason that our relationship failed if he was going to try. I got up and packed a bag. I jumped in the shower and got dressed to go.

The trip there was quiet. He would try to make conversation with me and I would come back with short answers. He didn't push too hard because he knew that I was doing good just to be going on this trip with him at this point. I sat there with my arms folded looking out the window at the scenery half the trip and the other half, I reclined my seat and fell asleep. Ordinarily when we would go on trips, I would stay up and keep him company while he drove and vice versa.

We arrived at the hotel and he walked inside to check in and came back with the key cards. It was a beautiful hotel, luxurious in fact. He grabbed his bag and I reached for mine "Don't you touch that bag, I got dis" he said as he grabbed my bag". We walked into the hotel and got on the elevator and went to the 8th floor. We stepped off walked down a few feet and he stopped at our room and opened the door. We walked into the room and there was a king-sized bed neatly made with rose petals scattered and two kissing dove figurines made from towels. There was a bottle of champagne sitting in a bucket of ice on the dresser along with two champagne flutes. It was hard to stay mad with him when he had gone through the trouble of setting this up. I couldn't make it easy for him though "Awww this is nice" I said.

He popped the cork on the champagne and filled the flutes then handed me one "here you go" he said as he handed the glass to me. I took the glass but was still hesitant to let everything go. "Cheers to new beginnings for us" he took his glass and clinked it against mine.

"Cheers"

We sipped on our champagne and then decided to walk out on the balcony to see the view. The view was breathtaking, the sound of the ocean was serene. The waves crashing as the water washed onto the shore. It had a way of making you forget about all your troubles, erasing all the blemishes from your past and melting your sorrows away. Kareem stood behind me and placed his hands on the balcony rail. He started to talk softly in my ear "You know I didn't mean anything that happened last night. I love you and I am so upset with myself for the way that I behaved."

"You should be."

He asked me to turn around, so I did. He looked me in my eyes and said "Alyssa, I love you and I mean that. You are my everything. I want us to get back to where we were in the beginning. I know I keep fucking up but I'm gonna get it right for you…for us." His words resonated with me because he wanted the same thing that I wanted, to get back to where we were. Somewhere we had gotten lost. I know that relationships are not always perfect. I expect to go through some bumps and bruises. We had certainly had our share but when do we say enough is enough? It was like we kept putting a band-aid on a wound that needed stiches. At any rate, I wanted to give him an opportunity to prove himself even if I had given him plenty chances before. It hadn't all been bad between us. We had some spectacular moments together. I didn't know what the future would hold but I was along for the ride. I believed that he loved me and that he was going to make some changes.

We took a stroll along the beach holding hands. The wind blowing through my hair and the wet sand creeping in between my toes. We conversed about what we wanted our futures to look like with each other. He vowed to be a better man than he had in the past. We dined in at an oceanfront restaurant. The food was amazing, and the view was spectacular. We laughed and enjoyed each other's company. It was like old times and I thought that this was growth for us. We needed this night to just tuck all our cares away for the moment. It was nothing sexual just quality time. Kareem never tried anything with me. I guess he just knew that I was not ready after the charade that he put on the night before. We laid in bed with the back door to the balcony open so that we could hear the peacefulness of the ocean. We drank champagne and fell asleep cuddling; something that we hadn't done in a while. I missed that feeling of laying in his muscular arms with him caressing my body tenderly. No sex, just two people connecting on a deeper level. It was a magical night, a night that I would not soon forget.

PRAY TOGETHER, STAY TOGETHER

The following Sunday we went to his childhood church. It was quite a distance from us, but I wasn't complaining. We walked hand in hand and sat down in the pew. The word seemed as if it was meant for us to hear. I loved how God worked in that way. When the preacher announced for people to come up and be saved even though we had both been saved at some point in our lives, we decided to go up and get saved together as a sign of unity before God. We stood there, hand in hand and let the preacher pray over us. It felt as though the weight that I had been carrying all this time had been lifted. For the first time in a long time I felt hopeful of our relationship. As we walked through the church after service let out, he began to introduce me to some of his old church family. Kareem introduced me as his fiancé to everyone we encountered. *Maybe just maybe we were heading in the right direction.* After all the hell I had been through, I was hoping that there was some light at the end of this tunnel. We began going to church every Sunday. Kareem was making progress. His attitude had shifted, and things were looking up. It was short lived though. It wasn't long before we ended up falling back into the same routine.

Suddenly Kareem went from working all the time to always looking for a job. He was just as inconsistent at working on our relationship and himself as he was at finding a career. When those red flags presented themselves, I should have run like hell but I'm a fighter. I don't throw in the towel that easily and at this point I was in way too deep. I wanted to be supportive rather than nag him for falling on hard times. I was just that type of woman.

Kareem began to complain to me that I needed friends citing that I had too much time on my hands. He thought that our issues came from the fact that I didn't have anyone to talk to and that I expected him to be there at all times. Truthfully, I did need someone to talk to. I had distanced myself from all my friends because they all saw through him and thought that I should leave him. I could not bring myself to do that. I wanted them to accept that he was my man. I would often justify his actions by saying that all relationships have problems, but the reality was, I was in denial.

Kareem introduced me to one of his female friends and her sister, they all hung out, drank and partied together. His friends name was Nicole and her sister named Tanesha, but he introduced her as Nesha, her nickname. I was leery at first, not understanding why he was introducing me to his female friends but, I thought *well at least he's not hiding it, so it must be strictly platonic.* Nicole and I instantly clicked. She was a cool chick who respected our relationship. She and I began spending a lot of time together. I talked to her about my issues with Kareem. She always listened and seemed to be understanding. She always reassured me that Kareem loved me and that he was a good guy. Although this was one of his friends, she and I had become very close ourselves. I was happy to have someone to vent to although I had to filter some things just to keep the peace, on the strength that it was his friend.

One day as we were riding to the mall, Nicole looked at me said "Alyssa, you have become my best friend, I feel like you and I are more like sisters than me and my own sister."

I was touched that she would say that, and quite frankly, she was the closet person that I had in my life. Nicole had been a shoulder for me to cry on, someone I could laugh with and we were inseparable. I even helped her get a job at the retail store that I worked at. We went to work together, we came home and hung out together. Nicole had become my best friend too.

"Nicole you have been a great friend to me and I consider you my best friend too, more like the sister I never had". Up until this point I had been isolated from everyone that I had ever knew and loved. I maintained my relationship with my parents, but I didn't feel like I could talk with them about the things that I was experiencing in this relationship. It felt good having a friend that he approved of and one that I had a bond with.

Unfortunately, as time passed the emotional and physical abuse only increased and there was still the same pattern of apology after apology. He began to put me down, calling me names, telling me I wasn't worth anything. Before I knew it, I had spent years of my life in this vicious cycle. I had become numb. It became so much a part of my life that I started to believe it. I think that is why I stayed with him and dealt with it all. I actually believed that I could not do any better than him and no one would want me. I believed him when he said that I was not that attractive, had no figure, had a dull personality, and I was not that smart. I mean *who would want to be with a woman like that?* I thought. I began to channel that energy inwardly and it showed. I emerged into an insecure woman therefore I had to do everything that I could to maintain my relationship with him. I tolerated the abuse, I overlooked the signs of him cheating, and I put everything I had into making him love me the way that he loved me in the beginning of our relationship.

Nicole tried to convince me that I was wrong, that I was beautiful inside and out. She didn't like the way that she saw him treat me, but she was torn because she was his friend too. She tried to just stay out of it and just encourage me to keep my head up.

Kareem and I were still sharing a car----my car which I paid for and he had most of the time. I rarely sat in the driver's seat of my own car. I paid most of the bills because of his inconsistencies with working and his lack of motivation to want anything better than what he had. Although, I did finish my undergraduate degree in sociology. I did not pursue my dreams of going to school to get my master's in social work. At some point, I began to question if I was smart enough to make it through a master's program. *Was I the counseling type?* I mean, I was having trouble managing my own life, how could I quiet possibly give advice on how to manage someone else's life? I continued working in retail and while I received higher pay for having a degree and I made decent money, it was not at all the life that I wanted for myself. I desired stability and when I expressed my concerns he only knocked me for it. He did not have any formal education and he worked little odd jobs here and there, but nothing was ever consistent. That may have worked for him when he was in his early twenties, but he was damn near 30. It was high time for him to make some career moves. You know start building our empire. It was almost as if he wanted to keep me at a certain level of success and he cared nothing about what my dreams were.

About two years after I graduated from college I found out that I was pregnant yet again. I was 24 years old which seemed to be a good age to start a family. However, I was still scared because...

well…the situation was not ideal to bring a child into but in some strange way I thought that if I could have this baby that it would somehow improve our relationship. After all, he was so happy when I told him of the last pregnancy. He was incredibly supportive and attentive. I would have given anything to get that from him again. The loss of my first pregnancy cut us both very deeply. It was a blow that neither of us ever really recovered from.

The first person I had to call was my best friend to share the news with her. Low and behold, Nicole announced to me that she was pregnant as well. I was thrilled, my best friend and I were going to have children together. I'm just saying, what are the odds? It seemed like an ideal situation. Nicole didn't seem as thrilled as I was about the situation.

One day Nicole came to the house in tears, I opened the door giving her a hug to console her "Hey boo, what's wrong? What's wrong Nicole? Talk to me".

"I'm not ready to be a mother, I am going to have an abortion".

I was shocked by this admission "Nicole NO, we are never really ready to become mothers, it's just something we do. We are going to have our kids together and be good mothers to our kids together. Our kids are going to grow up together. This is God's plan for us you can't do this."

She was adamant "Michael, the man that I am pregnant by has a wife and other children. When I told him, he let me know that he was married with children and that I could not have this baby. He said that if I did, he would have nothing to do it."

"Nicole, did you know that he was married?"

"I had no idea until he just told me, I am devastated."

"Well fuck him, he is an ain't shit type of dude, anyway. He lied to you and now you are having his baby, but you don't need him Nicole. You can do this on your own. Plenty of single women have babies and they do just fine. I got your back and I always will."

She hugged me and broke down in tears "Thank you so much for being a true friend to me." She decided to keep the life that was growing inside of her and we went through our pregnancy together. We shared stories about what was happening to our bodies as our bellies grew. As it turned out she was not the only one going through her pregnancy without the father, my pregnancy was a complete disaster. I became so ill with this pregnancy as it turned out, Kareem was not attentive at all. In fact, he was barely there. He was always working yet when it came time to pay bills he always had an excuse as to why he could not pay. I had the burden of all the financial responsibilities on my shoulders.

I had isolated myself from family because I knew that I could not discuss this with them. When you think of pregnancy, you think of a happy glowing woman whose man waits on her hand and foot because he doesn't want her to work too hard.

My pregnancy was not like that at all, I was far from glowing and he damn sure did not wait on me hand and foot. If anything, I was stressed out, working more than normal to make ends meet and preparing for the new life that we had coming into the world. I couldn't afford the cute maternity clothes, so I made due with bigger clothes that I brought from Goodwill. I kept my long hair in a ponytail because I could not afford to go to a salon regularly to get it done nor did I have the energy to do much more than that myself. I was miserable, uncomfortable and struggling financially. The only thing that kept me going was the eagerness of meeting my unborn child for the first time and the fact that my best friend and I were getting through this together.

CHANGING FACES

I was about 4 months pregnant and I was laying in the bed feeling sick as usual trying to keep my food down which had become a daily project. The phone rang, Nicole popped up on my caller Id. "Hello" I answered.

"Hey Alyssa, whatcha doing?"

I could sense something in her voice. She sounded nervous. "Nothing, I am just lying in the bed, girl you know I can't seem to keep anything down. Is everything okay?"

"No Alyssa, I really need to talk to you. It's very important. Is Kareem there?"

"No, he's at work, he won't be home until late tonight. He has to work security tonight at the club."

"Okay good, can I come over there?"

"Of course!"

"Ok I'm on my way, I will be there in 15 minutes."

The suspense was killing me. *What on earth could she have to talk to me about that was so important? What was making her so nervous to talk to me and why did she care if Kareem was home or not?* Finally, the doorbell rang, I got up off the bed and walked to the door.

"Hey Nicole" I said as I opened the door.

"Hey Alyssa" she said as she put her head down.

"What's going on Nicole, what did you need to talk to me about?" I did not want to wait any longer or prolong it with small talk.

"Well there is something that I have to tell you, but you can't tell Kareem that I am telling you this. Do you promise you won't say nothing?"

Now my heart was pounding, what could she quite possibly tell me about Kareem that we had not already discussed over the course of our friendship. "I promise." I said hesitantly.

"Ok you are going to need to sit down for this because what I have to say is going to be a lot for you to take in"

I sat down on the edge of the couch and took a deep breath. "ok go on spit it out already."

"Well let me start from the beginning. This has been eating at me and I just cannot keep it from you any longer." She took and deep breath and looked me in my eyes. "Before Kareem introduced me to you, he came to me and asked me to befriend you so that I could keep you busy. You know, basically to distract you from what he was doing. He told me you were crazy, and I believed him until I met you and got to know you. Then I realized, that you embodied the true definition of a good woman who was being taken through a lot of changes. He and I had a little thing going on, but it wasn't anything serious."

"Wait---what? What do you mean you had a thing going on?"

"We were fuck buddies, I knew about you but like I said he made it seem like you were just this crazy girl that he could not seem to shake off and it wasn't like I had feelings for him or anything. Once you and I became friends and I got to know you, I cut it off."

"So, let me get this straight, you are basically telling me that the only reason that we clicked the way that we did is because he enlisted you to be my friend?

"At first yes, but like I said when I got to know you I really liked you and I thought you were nothing like what he had described you as. You just loved your man and would do anything for him, there is nothing crazy about you. The more I hung around you, the more I realized he was the crazy one. Our friendship is genuine. You have been there for me more than my own family. You are my best friend Alyssa. You have to believe that."

"I don't know what to believe at this point. Is there anything else you want to tell me?" I said stoically. I was completely devoid of any emotions.

"It's just one more thing----When you were at work one night we ummm" she said clearing her throat.

"We ahhh what?"

"We had some drinks and one thing led to another. We had sex and now I don't know if…. I—I- I'm not sure if I am carrying his chil---"

"Wait. Stop. You think that you could be pregnant by Kareem?" You could probably feel the heat radiating off my body. This was too much for any one person to deal with, let alone a pregnant woman whose hormones were all over the place.

"Yes, I am sooooo sorry Alyssa" she said tearfully.

"What about the married man you were sleeping with was that a lie to cover this up?"

"No, that situation is real and now I don't know which one of them is the father. I got pregnant around the time that I was with Kareem, but I was with Michael around the same time. But the incident with Kareem was just a one-time thing---I mean since we had cut everything off a long time ago. Look Alyssa, you deserve better than him. You really need to leave him".

How the hell am I supposed to keep this a secret and why would I? I thought to myself. I mean I had just learned that my best friend was my best friend by design and that she was a bonified hoe sleeping with MY man who she now believed could be the father of her unborn child. And… we were pregnant at the same damn time. What loyalty did I have to this woman? She obviously had no loyalty to me. Who was this chick? The hurt that I felt at that moment was unbearable, indescribable and unconscionable.

"How dare you sit here and cry to me about this as if you are hurt. I'm the victim here and you are the culprit. If what you are saying is true, there is no way that we can go forward as friends and there is no way I am keeping this a secret. Get out! I want you to leave…RIGHT NOW. I can't even look at you right now and the only thing that is keeping me from beating your ass is the fact that we are both with child. You got some nerve."

"Alyssa don't do this. You promised."

"Fuck that! I promised my friend. You are not my friend. I don't know who you are. Now get out! I said as I escorted her to the door and slammed the door behind her.

I now had more to add to the issues that I had with Kareem. The problems just seemed to mount, and I debated on whether to discuss this with him or do as I had promised. It was an internal struggle because while I knew that this woman was not my friend I could not change the fact that I was loyal to a fault. If I made a promise, it was one I intended to keep but this was weighing on me heavily. Nicole knew that about me and perhaps that is why she made me promise before she revealed this information to me. I decided that this was one promise that I had to break for my own sanity. I had just lost my best friend and if this was true, I would lose my man too. I could not imagine a worse feeling. I felt ill, sick on my stomach but at this point I could not be sure whether it was a symptom of pregnancy, the stress I was feeling as a result of this admission or both. I would not wish this type of pain on my worst enemy.

I waited anxiously for Kareem to get home from work. This admission was festering in me like lava in a volcano waiting to erupt. There was no way I was going to get any rest until I addressed this.

Did Nicole really think that after telling me something of this magnitude I was just going to keep it a secret. She's out of her mind. *Clearly.*

Finally, I heard the key turn in the door knob and I jumped up to greet him at the door. "Hey Alyssa, what are you doing up?"

If looks could kill, he would be a dead man, "waiting on you, we need to talk NOW" I said with emphasis as I cut my eyes at him.

"Ok, what is it Alyssa? What is so important that we gotta talk about it at 4 o'clock in the morning? He said as he was looking at his watch.

I honestly didn't know where to start. Everything that I had rehearsed in mind went blank. I didn't know whether to break the promise that I made to the first person that came to me with accusations about him cheating, the second or huge bomb that my ex-best friend just dropped in my lap. I decided to leave the past in the past since I had not addressed it before now and just discuss the accusations that Nicole had just made. After all, I had more than enough ammunition with what Nicole told me. "I had a very interesting conversation with Nicole earlier today and she shared some pretty disturbing news with me. First off, she said that you asked her to befriend me to basically keep me out of your hair."

Kareem's mouth dropped, and I could see his temper flaring. "Say what?"

"Let me finish Kareem, there is much more to this accusation and I need to get it all out. She also said that y'all used to be fuck buddies and she slipped up with you not too long ago after a night of drinking and slept with you again and the baby she is carrying now may be yours."

"What the fuck? And let me guess you believe that dumb shit? She is a pathological liar! That bitch is just jealous of you and our relationship. She is mad because she is having a baby by a man who is married and don't want nothin' to do wit her. You are a fool if you believe her Alyssa."

"Why would I doubt such an accusation? Why would she lie about something like that?" I said crossly.

"She is a bitter ass, miserable ass black woman who does not want to see you or any other woman happy. Please don't tell me you going to let this woman come in and break up what we got going on. I know it isn't perfect, but we have been doing better. I love you, the only reason I bought her around is because I felt like you needed some friends. You had distanced yourself from your friends from high school because of me and I felt bad. It had nothing to do with me trying to get you out of my hair." By this time, he was ranting and raving. "I have never touched that girl and I can't believe she would stoop so low to try to break us up. I was like a brother to her. She ain't shit for this."

"She asked me not to mention it to you and I promised her I wouldn't before she told me what it was, but I couldn't keep that one in."

"That should have been clue number one that she was lying. She wanted you to leave me for something that you could not even discuss with me. That shit's crazy. She is crazier than I ever gave her credit for and to think that despite all that I still had her back. The reason she didn't want you to say anything is because she knows that she is lying. Please let's not forget she is the type of woman that will knowingly sleep with a married man and get pregnant on purpose.

Yes! I said it, on purpose. She got pregnant to try and trap that man and now that she sees it ain't working, she's fuckin miserable"

I was sitting there with question marks floating through my head. *Could she have been lying just to break us up?* I mean *why would she feel that it was a good time to tell me something like this after all the time that we had been friends for so long? Could I be wrong for believing her?* He is claiming that he never touched her. *Why would she want me to not tell him?* "I don't know what to believe right now Kareem."

"Let's call her tomorrow and have her sit down and discuss this like grown-ups, I bet she won't do it because she knows that she would not be able to maintain that lie. I'm done with her ass and you should be too. She is not your friend. But I am going to hash this out with her one way or another, with or without you and I would rather you be there so set that up later today." He rubbed my belly and said "You don't need to let this upset you and the baby. I can't believe she would do this while you were pregnant. She knows that you miscarried the first time you were pregnant right?"

"Yes, she knows."

"She ought to be ashamed, but I know she ain't. She is just foul. You know what if she doesn't want to sit down and talk about this, we can ask Nesha, she knows how foul her sister can be and that's her sister."

I never thought about asking her sister. I knew that her and her sister didn't have the best relationship, but I didn't really didn't talk to her sister like that. We were cool, but we never hung out or anything. Nicole had often talked about the fights that they had and how they would make up and be cool again, but they were never that close like I thought that we were. On the other hand, Kareem seemed to be closer to Nesha than to Nicole especially here recently. It would have seemed that if there was something going on between them that it would have been the other way around. Man, this was totally confusing. I just wanted the truth. But I couldn't very well base my decision on an accusation that was made with no justification or proof. If he had of admitted that there was a sexual relationship between them at some point that would be one thing, but he is denying everything and even willing to sit down and address this with her together. I knew that he could be charming, cunning in fact, but I was not the type to believe everything I heard. I needed proof especially when it involved something as serious as this.

"Come here." He said as we walked toward one another. "Don't let that girl get into your head and mess up what we are trying to build here. We will devise a plan to address this so that we can get to the bottom of this but in the meantime, I don't want you to be worried about it. There is no truth to it. Now, I want you to lay down and get some rest the baby needs you to. You know Monday we find out if it is a boy or a girl. But I know it's a boy."

I hesitantly laid down in the bed, but I was tired and confused. I just wanted to stop thinking for a little while. Kareem headed to the shower and I fell asleep. When I woke up, I sent Nicole a text *I need to talk to you ASAP, don't want to talk on the phone, let me know when you can come to the house.*

She texted right back *I can come now is* **Kareem** *there?*

I thought about telling the truth, Kareem was still lying in bed asleep, but I thought that if I told her the truth she would not come, and I would never get the answers that I so desperately needed.

No, he just left for work.

Ok, give me 1hr and I will be there.

I turned to Kareem and said "wake up, Nicole is on her way over here and we are going to get to the bottom of this. In a way I felt kind of bad knowing that she was going to be ambushed, not knowing that Kareem was there but another part of me didn't care because she had been putting on a façade throughout our "friendship". Kareem jumped up and said "good, I want her to tell that lie with me sitting right there".

We both got dressed and I went and sat on the couch. "Did you tell her I was here?"

"No, I told her you were at work."

"Well when she gets here I am going to wait in the back, when I hear the lies, I will come back up front" He was adamant that these were lies.

Nicole pulled up in the driveway and walked to the door. You could see her baby bump in the outline of her form fitting blue dress. Kareem did just we discussed and walked to the back. I opened the door "hey come on in".

She had a look of shame on her face. "Hey Alyssa, I was shocked to hear from you today. I hope that you didn't mention any of this to Kareem. He would never admit this anyway."

"Nicole, how could you sleep with my man, my child's father, knowing everything we have already been through?"

"Alyssa, I'm sorry, it just happened. It meant nothing to me and I don't think it meant anything to him either. We were drunk."

"What about the fact that y'all were fuck buddies while we were together, how could you be so cold and then befriend me?"

"We were friends with benefits long before I knew about you but like I said when I got to know you I cut it off."

"You cut what off Nicole?" Kareem said as he walked into the room.

"You set me up Alyssa?" Nicole said in shock.

"Nah fuck that set you up bullshit, you don't have to say another word Alyssa if this chick wanna lie on me she gonna have to do it to my face. You cut me off from what Nicole?

"I'm not getting ready to do this, I'm pregnant and I do not need this stress"

Kareem began to raise his voice "you brought this stress on yourself with these lies you filling Alyssa's head up with. You know damn well we never slept together. I never touched you. You may have wanted me to, but I never saw you in that way. You were like a sister to me and you lie on me like this. What's wrong you mad that the married dude you was fucking don't want anything to do with you?"

"Come on Kareem, that's not fair." She said shamefully.

"No what's not fair is what you were trying to do here. You wanted Alyssa to leave me so that she could be in the same boat with you, a miserable ass single mother." He said with disdain.

"Kareem, you know what the truth is but I'm not going to stand here and let you talk to me like this. You may be able to slap Alyssa around and disrespect her, but you won't do it to me. To hell with both of you. Alyssa, if you want to stay with this bum that has been cheating on you and disrespects you, then go ahead."

I sat there quiet because I had nothing to say. I was still trying to make sense of what was being said. He was outright denying the allegations and she was being dismissive. The only truth that I had heard is that Kareem had been disrespectful and there were certainly some allegations of cheating in the past. But I need something to substantiate the claims and as of right now we were working to get past the disrespect.

"Ok it's time for you to go Nicole." I said firmly.

"Yeah get the fuck out Nicole and take your lies with you" Kareem said smugly.

Nicole walked out the door she turned around and looked back me with a look of sympathy. I didn't know how to take any of this. I chose to sweep it under the rug just as I had done everything else.

'PEACHES'

The time had come for us to determine the sex of the baby. We walked into the doctor's holding hands. The waiting room filled with other pregnant women and their spouses or boyfriends. The atmosphere was relaxing and inviting. "Ms. Calloway" the nurse called. We got up and walked to the back with her. The nurse said "Ms. Calloway you need to take your shirt off and put this on. The ultrasound tech will be in with you in a moment". She handed me a blue paper vest that opened in the front and walked out of the room. Just as I got the vest on that the nurse provided me with and laid down on the table, we heard a knock at the door. "Ms. Calloway, hi I'm going to be doing your ultrasound today. Are you ready to find out what you are having?"

"Yes, we are" I said holding Kareem's hand and smiling.

"Great, let's get started" she pulled a bottle of blue gel out and warned me "this is going to be cold".

I was all too familiar with that feeling. She squirted it out on my rounded pregnant belly and pulled out the ultra sound instrument. Kareem and I both eagerly looked on the screen and you could see this little baby moving around. It was such a beautiful and amazing sight. "It's a girl" the ultrasound technician announced.

Kareem fell out of the chair "a girl? I am having a little girl?"

"Why are you so surprised Kareem?" I asked as I let out a chuckle.

"I just thought it was gonna be boy"

"Well she is a girl, now we can start picking out names for HER." I emphasized.

I was filled with excitement, it was a little girl. I couldn't wait to see her little face. A little girl, wow! I get to buy little cute outfits and do her hair real pretty and teach her all the things that she would need to know about being a woman.

I was nervous throughout my pregnancy because I was always scared to miscarry and as much strain as I had put on my body because I was doing everything myself I was shocked but thankful that I had made it this far. But you can't interfere with God's plan. I made it through my entire pregnancy although I went into preterm labor at 34 weeks. I went to the hospital and they were able to stop the contractions. I was placed on bedrest for the remainder of my pregnancy and I ended up having my daughter Alexis at 38 weeks, still slightly early but not early enough to be considered premature. My parents were there to witness the birth and they instantly fell in love with her just like I had. I saw the excitement on their faces. My mom held her in her arms for the first time and displayed a look of pride. My father snapped picture after picture, capturing every moment. They cherished their first and only granddaughter and they made it evident as the days passed. My mom came home with me when they released me from the hospital to help me with Alexis. She woke up in the middle of the night and helped with feedings. My dad came by almost every day to check on us. My parents and I were reconnecting, and I couldn't be happier.

For about the first 3 months after Alexis was born, I saw a shift in how Kareem treated me. He became the man that I fell in love with and I thought we would have a happy family and live happily ever after. Things were beginning to look up----AGAIN. My daughter was here, and she was so very important to me. She was absolutely beautiful, she had the cutest little button nose, big brown eyes, long eyelashes, a head full of straight black hair and a caramel complexion. I wanted to give her the world and teach her all things that she would need to know to be successful in life. That meant that I would have to make some changes of my own. I had to learn to value myself and put myself first for a change. I think that throughout the course of our relationship with all the ups and downs, I had lost myself somewhere along the line.

I could not very well be a strong example for my daughter if she grew up seeing me being cheated on emotionally and physically abused by her father. I loved him, and I had a great deal of time and emotional energy invested in him, but I had also built myself back up mentally and spiritually and I knew that something needed to change. I may not have been where I needed to be; but I was seeing things differently. All his past infractions began swirling in my mind. *Did he have another girlfriend when we first started dating? Did he cheat on me throughout our relationship? Did he sleep with my best friend? Was the baby she was carrying his?* I no longer felt an obligation to make things work between us because of the time. I knew it was not God's plan for my life to have to stay with a man that I essentially did not trust. I was proud of him for making the changes that he had made and working to keep us together as a family unit for right now but how long would it last? We had so many ups and downs and to be honest it was mostly downs. No sooner than I could process these thoughts, everything came crashing down around me.

The final breaking point with Kareem came when an incident between he and I had gone way too far, and the truth spilled out about all his indiscretions while we were together. Alexis was about 6 months old, I was at home listening to the radio as I did when I was at home just relaxing. It was late night and people were calling in to give shout outs which was usually pretty funny to me however this time I did not see the humor. A lady by the name of "Peaches" called in to give her man an anniversary shout-out and coincidentally his name was Kareem. She even named his place of employment which happened to be the same as Kareem's place of employment. Suddenly, this did not feel like a coincidence anymore.

I knew that something was off about this and I intended to get down to the bottom of it. No longer would I stand by and brush things under the rug. I decided I would do some of my own investigating and in that moment, I became inspector gadget. I shuffled through papers in our bedroom looking for anything out of the ordinary. I looked in pockets of his clothes trying to find the least little clue and finally I thought *if he is dealing with someone else, he must be calling them on the phone.* It was one of those *Ah-hah* moments. I began by looking through phone records, checking for numbers that he called frequently and that called him frequently and *BAM*, this one number sticks out like a sore thumb on his call detail. I mean he spent hours on the phone with this person during times that he should have been at work. It was the only number on his call detail that that showed up frequently that I didn't recognize. Since I was one of those type of women that needed proof to make a decision to leave, it was proof I intended to get. Everything in my gut was telling me that something just wasn't quite right even though things had been on the up and up lately. Kareem was slick, and I knew that about him, but my women's intuitions was setting off alarms. I decided I was going to call the number. The phone rang, and a woman answered the phone "Hello".

"Hello, may I speak with -------Peaches?" I went for it, what did I have to lose. Hell, I can be slick too. I may have been a fool, but I am no dummy.

"This is Peaches, who is this?" *Bingo!* I thought to myself.

"Peaches this is Alyssa, you don't know me, but I think that I just heard you just make a shout out on the radio to Kareem"

"Yes, I did, are you calling from the radio station?"

"No, I know that this is odd but from one woman to another I am just curious if his name is Kareem Anderson?"

"Yes, where are you calling me from again?" She seemed like a reasonable woman. I held nothing against her, despite the shock that I was experiencing considering she had just revealed that she had given an anniversary shout out on the radio for her boyfriend which also happened to be my boyfriend and daughter's father. Truth is in that moment, I was not angry. In a sense, I felt relieved to now have proof that he had been cheating and disappointed in myself for staying in a situation like this for as long as I had. My only hope is that when all was said and done that he would be a good father.

I wanted this to be cordial, I was a mother and I wanted to represent myself as such. "As I said before, my name is Alyssa, I know that this is going to sound strange, but I would like to sit down and talk with you face to face."

"About what?"

"Your boyfriend Kareem and my boyfriend Kareem"

"Wait, What? What do you mean?" I heard a variety of different emotions in her voice and they all sounded familiar to me. I was not trying to hurt her, I knew what that felt like all too well. I just wanted to handle this situation like a civilized woman and I felt that she had the right to know. I only hoped that she could be equally reasonable.

"I just had a baby by Kareem 6 months ago and we have been living together for years."

"Years? We have been together for the last year it was our anniversary today." She sounded it as though she was stunned and confused but eager to know more.

"I kind of gathered that from your shout out on the radio, which is what prompted me to do some further investigating. Listen, I know that this is a hard pill to swallow but would you mind meeting with me.

To my surprise she was very accommodating and asked to meet me out for lunch the following day. "Yes, let's do lunch and do me a favor let's not mention this to Kareem just yet. I would like to sit with you first and get a better understanding of what is going on here.

"No problem, can we meet at 1pm tomorrow at Kelly's Café, you know where that is right?"

"Yes, I do, and I will be there." She said eagerly.

The following day, I pulled up to the restaurant I did not know who to look for other than her name was Peaches. I stood outside the building holding my daughter in her carrier. A woman approached and said, "Hey is your name Alyssa?"

"Yes, you must be Peaches" I extended my hand and we shook hands. There was no point in being upset with this woman who knew nothing about me and I knew nothing about her. The way I saw it we were just two women who had been played by the same man. We sat down at our table and she just glanced over at my daughter in an awkward silence.

"So, Peaches, I know that this is difficult, but I just needed to know if you ever had any suspicions that he may have been seeing anyone else."

"No, we spend most of our free time together, I work a lot, so I am not always available. I would have never thought that he would be disloyal though. He just did not strike me as the type."

"Me either, I would have never thought that he would either when we first started dating but he has been showing me a different side of him lately. I wanted to bring you some proof of our relationship just so know that I am not making any of this up. I am not here to hurt you only bring you the truth. What you choose to do with it is completely up to you. I have already decided that I am leaving. I have a daughter now and there is no way that I can tolerate this type of behavior from him and be a good influence on her"
"Okay, I understand. Well I see the little girl you share, and I see a lot of resemblance to him which I did not know that he had so that's strike one."

I pulled out pictures of us together when I was pregnant with Alexis and of us in the hospital together when Alexis was born. In one photograph he and I shared a kiss as we held our baby girl together. I also showed her text messages in my phone from him. With each item that I revealed to her she became more and more upset. Not with me but with him and I could see the pained look on her face. I sat there with her for a while and just discussed some things with her concerning Kareem. She was very polite and said to me "I hope you don't mind but I invited Kareem here for lunch. He does not know that you will be here of course. I find that the element of surprise is always the best way to discover the truth. I hope you won't leave. I don't want to turn this into a spectacle because I am too classy for that, but I want him to know why I am leaving him. I told him to get here at 1:45pm which is in a few minutes my plan is to have you go to the bathroom and come out when he is sitting down with me."

"I like the way you think. I think that is a wonderful idea." We were both sitting close to the window and I could see his car approaching the restaurant.

"There he is. He is about to turn into the parking lot. I hope he does not recognize my car. I parked on the side maybe he will not park over there." I grabbed Alexis in the carrier and walked toward the bathroom. As I passed by our waitress I let her know that another guest would be joining us but not to let him know that it was a party of 3 that he was sitting at. She looked at me strange but she told me that it was not a problem.

I took a moment to change my daughter's diaper figuring that would give him enough time to come in and settle down in the seat. As I walked out of the bathroom, I peeked around the corner to ensure that he was sitting and sure enough he had just come in kissed her and had sat down across from her. He was holding her hand and looking at her affectionately similar to the way that he used to look at me in the early stages of dating. I circled back around so that I could approach the table from behind so that he would not see me coming.

Once I approached, I tapped him on his shoulder. He looked back and looked at me as if he had seen a ghost. He snatched his hands out away from Peaches and said "Alyssa, what are you doing here?"

"I was wondering the same about you. So, who is this you are sitting with?"

He looked back at Peaches and she looked back at him "well aren't you gonna answer?" she asked.

He was speechless. It was almost as if a cat had snatched his tongue right out of his mouth.

Peaches decided to speak up "I am his girlfriend, nice to meet you and you are?" Kareem put his head down and his hand over his face.

"I am Kareem's fiancé, and this is our daughter Alexis. Kareem is there a reason why this woman would say that she is your girlfriend. Does she know that we live together and have been living together for quite some time?" I said fiancé because he had asked me to marry him although he never gave me a ring and we never set a date, I wanted the extent of our relationship to be well known.

Kareem's only response was to get up and leave. Deep down, I knew that would be his response. He was caught red handed. There was no way to explain this away. He would have to wallow in the consequences. "Wait! Where are you going Kareem?" Peaches said to Kareem, but he just kept walking out the door as if he were deaf. It was not important to me what Peaches was going to do with her relationship with Kareem. I was only concerned with what I would do with myself and my daughter. Peaches said to me as she extended her hand "Thank you for making me aware and you have a beautiful baby girl together. I hope everything works out for you but honey I'm done with this."

I shook her hand and thanked her for the opportunity to come out meet with me and wished her the best of luck. We parted ways. I took Alexis home and began to pack his things in boxes. This was the last straw. There was no way after having physical proof of his infidelities that I would stick around. I did not know where he was going to stay, and I did not care. I only knew that he would not spend another night under the same roof as me. He had been with this woman for a good majority of our relationship. He had been emotionally and physically abusive toward me and I was not taking it anymore. I finally had the proof that I needed to gain the strength to leave.

DAZED AND CONFUSED

I heard the door open and Kareem walked in with his signature flowers and a card.

"Alyssa, listen to me, I can explain" I took the flowers and card and threw them directly in the trash can.

"No, you can't, you cannot make this right again. We are through. Did your other girlfriend leave you too? Is that why you are here with your sob story?"

Kareem became infuriated, it was as though his eyes glazed over, and he transformed into a different person. "Alyssa, I am not going anywhere, and neither are you. You are definitely not taking my daughter outta here." He shouted.

"Shhhh…. You are going to wake Alexis, lower your voice and yes you are leaving…. tonight. I don't care where you go but there is nothing to work on here. All I get from you is your tired ass apologies. I am done with this. I deserve more than that. I have been nothing but good to you."

"I am not going anywhere" He shouted angrily.

"Oh really" I said as I reached for the phone. "Well if you won't leave willingly I will call the police and have you escorted away from here. Before I could get to the phone he snatched it back and threw it on the ground shattering the phone. Suddenly, I felt as though I was in danger, his temper was bursting out and I knew that he had no problems putting his hands on me when he was in that state.

"Get out of my way Kareem, I will just take the baby and leave myself."

He grabbed me by my arms and threw me down to the ground. "I told you, you are not going anywhere with my daughter"

"Kareem why are you doing this?" I began sobbing

Kareem slapped me in my face and said, "you are doing this to yourself".

He straddled his body over me as I struggled to get from under his weight. He placed his hand over my mouth and yelled "Shut up, I told you, you ain't going nowhere". He wrapped his hands around my throat and I began to fight harder. The harder I fought, the less I could breathe. I could feel a tingly sensation in my face and it felt as though I was getting ready to blackout. I saw my life flash before my eyes and I thought to myself, *this is it, he is going to kill me*. In that moment, I prayed to God that he would spare my life. Just as the darkness was setting in, he released his grip. I laid there coughing, trying to catch my breath. I was completely horrified. I was not a weak person by any stretch of the imagination, but I knew that if I came after him, he would kill me. He stood over me and said, "You are not worth keeping anyway". He spat on me, he turned away, walked out and slammed door. I got up, stumbled to the door and locked it behind him. I was humiliated and most of all I was mortified.

It was in this very moment that I began to question everything that I was ever taught about valuing myself. I felt worthless, I felt shame. I was so full of emotions. I desperately tried to gather my thoughts. I realized that locking the door would not keep him out because he had a key. I waited a few minutes and I ran into Alexis's room and gently grabbed her out of her crib and placed her in her carrier. I could not help but kiss her sweet face because for a moment in time, I thought that I would not see her again. I walked to my next-door neighbor's house and asked if I could use her phone. I was in tears and she could see that I had been in a physical altercation. I had marks on my neck and my face was bruised where he had slapped me. My hair and clothes were disheveled. I was a mess. She allowed me to come in and use the phone and I called 9-1-1. The 9-1-1 operator came on the line "9-1-1 what is your emergency?"

"Yes, my boyfriend just assaulted me, and I am scared to leave. I am scared that he may be waiting for me outside and he may harm me again. He tried to kill me!" I whimpered.

"What is your address ma'am?"

"1424 Grissle Lane, please send someone quick!"

"Someone will be there shortly to assist you ma'am. Please stay on the line with me until help arrives."

I did not have to wait long the police were there in a matter of minutes. They came in and took a statement from me. They advised me that I would have to go to the precinct in order to file charges against him since he was not there. I just wanted to get out of the situation, but I did not want to have him in any trouble with the law after all, he was the father of my child and I did not want to go through all the changes of going through court proceedings. I politely asked the officers if they could just escort me to my car with my things and that I would have the door locks changed the following day so that he could not get in. They were happy to oblige although they strongly encouraged me to reconsider pressing charges. I assured the officers that I simply wanted to get my daughter and I to a safe place and I would consider pressing charges then.

I didn't have a plan though and truthfully, I was scared to go back into my house. I couldn't very well stay at my neighbor's house with Alexis and I didn't have anywhere else to go. If I called my parents at this hour to ask them if I could stay with them, they would know something was wrong and I would have to explain but I didn't have a choice. I was nervous to call them, and I knew what my father's reaction would be as protective as he was over me and especially his newborn granddaughter. I had to do it though, the police had left, and I was running out of time to sit on my neighbor's couch whom I had never said anything more than "hey how are you" to. I picked up the phone and dialed my parents number. I was shaking when I heard my father's voice on the other end of the phone "Yello".

"Hey Dad."

"Hey baby girl, is everything alright, is Alexis ok?"

"Alexis is great, but…."

"But what?" He asked.

"I uhhh need to com—come and stay with you and mom for a

little while. Can you come and get me? I'm uhhh at my next-door neighbor's house." I said tearfully.

"Your neighbor's house? Alyssa what's going on?" He asked.

"I can't get into that right now. I just need you to come as soon as possible."

"I'm on my way." Click. He hung up and within 15 minutes I saw the headlights pull into my yard. I walked outside and ran to him and gave him a big hug. He glanced over me and saw that it looked as if I had been in a fight. "Alyssa, what the hell is going on? Are those bruises on your neck?"

I did not know how to answer because I knew that my father had a temper of his own and if he had an inkling that Kareem had done this to me, he would have his head on platter. I also could not lie to him. "Me and Kareem got into an altercation, I had to leave him, and I don't want to go back in that house. I don't know what he is capable of."

"That sonnava bitch, I'm going to kill that motherfucker.... where is he?" He headed towards the front door to open it and looked inside.

"Dad he left, he's not here. I need to go back over to the neighbors and get Alexis. I will be right back. Just wait here. I need to pack a bag so that I can stay with you tonight."

"Ok hurry back, I will stand right here and watch. If that sonnava bitch comes back here tonight he's going to have to deal with me." My dad was in excellent shape and he was built like Ving Rhames. He was a boxer in his younger days and he was known as the "chosen one" mainly because most felt that he was chosen to fight, he had a gift and it only took ONE hit to knock his opponent out cold. The last thing I wanted was for my father to get into a physical altercation with Kareem. I rushed back over to my neighbor's house grabbed Alexis in her carrier and rushed back over to my house. I packed a bag and got the hell out of there. I knew that there would be more questions to come and I thought that the ride back home would be when those questions would be asked but instead he never uttered a word to me. I guess he was contemplating what he was going to do to Kareem when he saw him again.

When we arrived at the house I was exhausted, all I wanted to do was take a shower and get Alexis in a comfortable place to sleep and lay down myself. My mom was in the bed and apparently had no idea of what was going on and I had hoped to keep it that way at least for the moment. And that's exactly what I did.

The next morning, I went to the real estate office to find out what I could do to get out of my lease so that I could move to a safer place. I explained the incident to them and they were more than willing to allow me to move out as soon as I needed to. I moved out of the house and moved in with my parents a short time later without any other incidents. It was different living with my parents after being on my own with Kareem for so long. It took some getting used to although I was thrilled to have the extra help full time. I did not have to worry about paying childcare because my mother was always willing to keep Alexis while I worked.

Months passed, and I had not seen or heard from Kareem. I could have personally done without seeing or hearing from him, but our daughter needed her father. A part of me wanted him to stay away from her because I saw his violent side first hand and it made me worry about leaving her alone with him. The other part of me remembered the softer side and I simply wanted him to be the type of father that Alexis deserved. My father wanted me to have nothing to do with Kareem, but I could not find it in myself to block him for seeing Alexis. As it turned out, I didn't have to, Kareem refused to see his daughter because I called the police on him as if I had no reason to. Instead of being remorseful for his actions that night he became resentful towards me and he took it out on our daughter. He would not tell me this directly, he would pass messages through our mutual acquaintances.

After all that had happened, there was one thing that seemed to haunt me and that was the issue with Kareem and my ex-best friend. She had warned me to leave him and accused him of possibly fathering her child and now I was wandering how she was doing. She should have had her baby too and the curiosity was taking its toll on me. I decided that I would offer and olive branch to Nicole. I missed having someone to talk to and even though I was still angry with her, I had to admit that I still cared about her. I picked up the phone and dialed her number, to my surprise she answered. It sounded as he if she was trying to hurry up and pick up the phone "Hellllo".

"Nicole, this is Alyssa."

"I know…. How are you Alyssa?"

I am doing good, I had a baby girl September 10th, I know you had your baby too, what did you have?"

"I had a little boy; his name is Kyree" I could hear her smiling through the phone. We talked as though nothing had ever happened, like we just picked up where we left off when time were good.

"Alyssa, I'm really sorry for hurting you. I made some bad

choices, but Kyree has changed my life."

"I know what you mean, so has Alexis. I accept your apology. I am just glad that chapter of my life is over. I would love to meet Kyree". A part of me wanted to meet Kyree to see if he resembled Kareem and the other part of me just wanted my friend back.

"You should come through, I will be home all day today." She said with excitement.

"Ok, I will be there in an hour, let me get Alexis together and I will head over there." I was nervous about seeing Nicole for the first time after we had that blow out. I was still hurt by the accusations but given my current circumstances with Kareem, it was worth me getting her full side of the story. She could have very well been telling the truth and if she had I still would have some reservations about forgiving her. The entire drive to her house all I could think was *why am I doing this? Am I just gluttoned for punishment?* I pulled up into her apartment complex, got out the car and pulled Alexis out in her carrier. I walked up the stairs to the second floor and approached her door. *Knock Knock,* I tapped on the door gently. Nicole opened the door and said, "Hey Alyssa, oh my God is this the baby, let me see her." She pulled the blanket of the top of the carrier, I usually kept her covered to keep the cool air from hitting her. When she pulled the cover off she was absolutely speechless, it was like she was frozen in time. "Ummm, she is beautiful, what is her name?"

"Alexis" I said proudly. "Where is lil Kyree, I can't wait to meet him" I was still unsure as to why Nicole had reacted like that when she saw Alexis for the first time

"He is in the living room in his crib, I think he may still be sleeping". Just then, we heard a baby crying over the baby monitor. "Well it looks like he's up, let me go get him." She walked back to the back for a few moments and came back out with him. They were almost exact same age only about 1 month apart and he was the oldest. His back was facing me when she walked out.

"Can I hold him?"

"Sure" She turned him toward me and I cradled him in my arms. I got a good view of his face and I was in complete shock. He and Alexis looked like they could be brother and sister. I mean they looked just alike. The resemblance was uncanny. "He is such a handsome little fella."

"Thank you." We both looked at each other like we knew what was coming next.

"You know they look a lot alike. Have you had a paternity test done yet?" I asked bluntly. She walked to the back and came back up front and handed me some papers. I unfolded the papers and read the bolded print: **Kareem D. Anderson --------------------99.9% biological father   Child--------Kyree J. Scott.**

"Wait, so you were telling me the truth the whole time? Kareem really is the father!" I exclaimed. The news just blew my mind, I felt light headed and I needed to sit down.

In the blink of an eye, I learned that my daughter has a big brother whose mother used to be my best friend. "I told you I wasn't lying, Kareem was a low down dirty dog! Yes, I was wrong for slipping up with him that time when we were drinking but I was not in my right mind. I would have never done that to you sober. I promise that when I became friends with you I ended things with him because it was never anything serious. I was young, dumb and horny and he was a good time. I just wanted to be honest with you when I revealed it to you. When he set everything up, he made it seem like the two of you were not that serious and he just wanted me to get you out of his hair. After conversations with you, I realized how good of a woman you were and that he was a liar and I cut him off. I know you had to notice that I stopped hanging out with him and started spending more time with you. It was because I realized that you were a good person.... a good friend and we just clicked. I never wanted to lose you as a friend, but I felt that this mistake was too deep to hide. But it was just that a mistake-----a mistake that I will regret for the rest of my life. The only good thing that came out of this was Kyree. He has changed my life so much."

I was speechless. While I was still trying to gain my composure, I listened intently to her every word. How does one forgive their friend for such an indiscretion and carry on the friendship like nothing ever happened? The fact remained that Kyree and Alexis are brother and sister and that was not going to change. "So, he knew all the time too, for him to have agreed to take a paternity test?"

"He sure did. I knew that he would never admit it, he wanted me to just pretend that it was Michael's baby and that he didn't want anything to do with us because he was married. He had me convinced that if I told you, you would hate me, and you probably do but it was just something I couldn't live with. I had to come clean."

"Does he see Kyree?"

"Nope, he wants nothing to do with either of us, but he does have to pay child support now" she said emphatically. *Who was this man? And what other secrets was he hiding?* I thought to myself. He didn't want anything to do with Alexis either simply because he did not want to deal with me. *Jack ass. How on earth did I find myself in this position?* I am a forgiving person by nature and I had come over there with full intentions on forgiving and forgetting the past and reconnecting with her. I knew that things would be awkward at first, but I had no idea that this was going to be the outcome. Here was yet more proof that Kareem was cheating and being deceitful not that I needed any more proof because I was done! I was too young, too beautiful and too good of a woman to tolerate any more of his bullshit. In the interest of our children, I thought it was best to be on my grown woman-ish and figure out a way to keep them in one another's lives. I knew that I could forgive but there was no way that we would ever be as tight as we once were. Hell, I couldn't even trust her around my man, if I should ever meet another. It was going to take some time for me to digest all of this, but the reality is that it was not going to change so I had to learn to accept it.

BACK TO JAIDEN

After Kareem and I separated it took a long time for me to begin dating again. For the first year or so, I focused solely on raising my daughter. After all, being a single parent was a difficult job. I began trying to repair relationships with my family and friends which I had distanced myself from because of this relationship. Nicole and I were cordial with one another and we brought the kids together for playdates. I appreciated her for being a grown woman about the situation and not acting like some of these other women who don't consider the child first and I am sure she thought the same about me. We both understood that our children did not ask to be here, and they deserved to grow up knowing their siblings. I was in a good place mentally and emotionally.

Over the next couple of years, I dated and found that there was nobody out there that captured my attention. It became kind of depressing. It was at this time that I decided to simply focus on me and my daughter and become celibate. I remained celibate for three years. I was too afraid to date because I was tired of the games that were played routinely, and I did not want to give into temptation considering I was not having sex. It was difficult at first, but it became easy for me when I reminded myself of my experience with Kareem. I learned valuable lessons from Kareem and I intended to use them going forward.

I began working toward goals that I had set for myself when I was a teenager. I was in the master's program and doing well having been inducted in to the National Honor Society. My success with school came as no surprise to me, school had always come easy to me. Don't get me wrong, it was hard work, but I have always enjoyed learning new things, reading and writing research papers, you know the things that most people hated about school. I seemed to be different from most, while others enjoyed the social experiences in school, I was more withdrawn and shied away from people and events where there were a lot of people. I had become an introvert. I put up this shield of protection around me. I did not want to make new friends because I had been seriously emotionally scarred by the one friend that I once held so dear to me and I did not want to be a relationship because my last one ended in disaster. I could not handle any more hurt and I wasn't ready to trust again. For the most part it was just me and Alexis and quite frankly, I didn't have time for anything else. Alexis kept me busy, I had to work, go to school, spend quality time with her and attend to her every need.

There was a part of me that wanted to have a father figure for Alexis. I grew up in a two-parent family and I wanted her to have the same experience. It became obvious over the years that Kareem was unwilling to step up and take on his responsibilities. We lived in the same town and he had only seen her maybe three times in passing. I had heard rumors around town through our mutual acquaintances that I had been keeping Alexis from him. Imagine that. Me the woman who is currently keeping in contact with the woman who laid down with my boyfriend, got pregnant, and had a baby for him; for the sake of the kids, keeping her father from seeing her. I never entertained those conversations, I realized that they had formulated their opinions about the situation based on accusations made from a man who was very cunning. Hell, he managed to perpetrate and defraud a whole lot of people along the way, so I wasn't really surprised that he had people believing these lies. Besides, what they thought about me didn't really matter. I knew who I was, and I knew that even after everything that he had put me through that I would never stop him from being a father to our daughter.... never.

Before I knew it, time had flown by. I was nearing the end of my last three classes and I would be done with school for good. My academic goals would be met, and I could go forward with my career goals. I was studying hard to pass the licensure board examination which I would need to take upon graduation. I had reestablished my independence. Finally, my dreams were within reach and I did not have the stress of trying to get my man to love me back. I had the love of my daughter and it was pure; it was real, and I did not have to do anything but be myself. She gave me the strength that I needed to be the best that I could be. She pushed me without having to say a word. She was my driving force.

I was excited to be approaching this major milestone in my life and for Alexis to witness me walking across that stage to receive my master's degree. It was the example that I wanted to set for her. I wanted her to know that if you put your mind to it you can achieve anything. I had been working a great job making good money working with troubled youth which gave me terrific experience. I was at a time in my life where nothing could stop me, sure as hell not a man. I did not have to pay attention to anyone's red flags because I played by my own rules. I was free, but little did I know that soon after I graduated my love life would soon take a dramatic turn.

I had been communicating with Jaiden now for the last three months. Jaiden was in Iraq on deployment and I was still playing hard to get. I felt the need to put my feelings in neutral to avoid getting hurt. I didn't want to rush into anything and I was still skeptical about having a long-distance relationship or any relationship at all. Jaiden on the other hand, seems to be in quite a rush. Jaiden was very persistent when we conversed, in trying to get me to enter a committed relationship with him. Red flag! He had mentioned marriage on our first date. Red Flag! Even with all the skepticism, I ignored all the red flags because I began to enjoy having the companionship of a man and the fact that he was at a safe distance made it easier for me. We spoke on the phone daily for hours. There was a huge time difference and he would generally call me when he got off work or before he went into work. That would mean that it was close to midnight when he would call me, I wasn't getting any rest, but I enjoyed our conversations.

It was about midnight when my phone rang. I kept my cell phone right near my head as I slept at night because I did not want to miss his call each night. The ringtone woke me, and I answered with a raspy voice "Hello" I said, clearing my throat.

"Hello beautiful, you know I hate waking you up, but I love to hear your voice"

"I don't mind waking up and talking to you"

"I miss you"

I got quiet, I did not know how to respond. I did not want to tell him that I missed him too because that would make me seem vulnerable and weak. How could he miss me he had only known me for few months or so and much of that was long distance. I had a difficult time understanding his need to push me into a relationship with him. After the experience that I had with my daughter's father, I wanted to take my time. I wanted to build a friendship first which is something that I did not do with her father. I felt that that it was important to build a solid foundation in order to have a healthy relationship. I had to admit, I did miss him, but I would never tell him that.

"Why are you so quiet" he said

"No reason"

"You don't miss me?"

"I miss being able to spend time with you and getting to know you" I said hesitantly.

"You don't feel like we have gotten to know each other? We spend hours on the phone sharing details about our lives. I feel as though, I am falling in love with you and want you to be with me."

"Be with me?" I asked.

"Yes, I want you to be mine"

"I don't think we should rush into anything. Let's continue to get to know one another before we enter into a committed relationship."

"Alyssa, I know what I want. I have never met anyone like you and I cannot imagine my life without you in it."

His words certainly made my heart melt. I wanted to be loved, most of all I deserved to be loved. I deserved to have a man in my life who would put forth as much effort as I would and love me unconditionally. He was offering to do that with me, yet I had some reservations. Something did not feel right. I needed more time to process. I did not want to live in a fairytale land that resulted in a nightmare. I had been down that road before and it was a long windy road that ended on a cliff. I quickly changed the subject. "How was your day?"

"It was good, I had to work a little later today. Can I do a video call with you? I just want to see your face."

"Okay call me back on Tango."

We disconnected the call and he called right back on the video chat app. "Hey!"

The picture was grainy and dark, but I could see that beautiful smile and it made my heart melt.

"Wow, you are gorgeous even when you just wake up, just flawless."

Of course, I was blushing from ear to ear. When I was with my daughter's father, all I ever heard were complaints about my appearance. It did not matter what time of day he saw me, I was never good enough for him. In the beginning of our relationship, he complimented me but once we were in a relationship he slowly moved to the insults. My self-esteem took a major hit as a result and it took a long time for me to feel good about myself again. It was refreshing to hear someone be so vocal on my features and making me feel beautiful again.

"Thank you, I am loving that smile you are wearing."

"Thank you gorgeous, no one brings it out better than you."

"Awww."

"How's Alexis doing" I loved that he asked about my daughter. That was important to me because if he wanted to be with me, he had to be willing to have a relationship with my daughter. That is non-negotiable.

He never ceased to amaze me. His words were like gold to me, but I knew that I had to be strong. I wanted to be friends first and build a solid foundation and he wanted to just enter into a relationship. We continued our conversation on the phone just discussing his day and my day at work. We laughed and laughed until I had to get off the phone. I had to get some sleep before I had to go into work. I looked at the clock and it was 2:02 am. I had to be up at 6:30 am to prepare for work and get my daughter ready for school.

Later that day

"Alyssa there is something up front for you" said the Sheila. Sheila was the receptionist in the office where I worked. I walked up front to see what she was referring to and as I approach her desk, I see a huge bouquet of roses. They were beautiful red roses in a stunning arrangement.

"Those are for me?" I asked

"Yes, they just came in" she said. You could tell that she wanted to be nosey and look at the card.

Who are they from? My first instinct was that they were from Jaiden, but I had only disclosed with him where I worked at once and I never gave him the address. He would literally have to had done some research to figure that out. *Impressive.* I thought to myself. The women in the office all gathered around me to see what was going on. I had the biggest smile on my face and I could not contain it. I had never received flowers at my job, as crazy as it sounds. My daughter's father never did anything like that before. I suppose he set the standard for all other relationships that I would enter, so anything outside of that was remarkable. I pulled the card out and read it silently to myself. It read ***"Yellow roses symbolize friendship; these roses are red so how do you think I feel about you?"***

"Let me see" said Vanessa.

I handed her the card and she read it silently "oh my God, this man is in love with you. What did you do to this man before he left? She said giving me the side eye.

"I didn't do anything to him or with him, I swear" I said as I raised my hand up. She and I walked back into the office that we shared, and I placed the flowers on my desk. I looked at them with adoration. It was gesture that had completely moved me. Some would say it was naivety and presently I would have to agree but at this time I was beginning to let down those walls down that I had up for so long.

"Do you really think that he is in love with me?"

"Alyssa, he obviously has some strong feelings for you"

"He wants to be in a relationship with me like right now, but I feel like we are moving too fast"

"Alyssa, give this man a chance, you have been wanting a good man to come along and treat you the way that you deserve to be treated. He is doing and saying all the right things. Don't let him get away from you because you may push him away."

"I get what you are saying but why can't we just be friends or talk until we are both ready to pursue a relationship. I don't want a long-distance relationship. I have communicated that to him. I just want to stay in contact with him and perhaps we will know each other well enough in the time that he is gone to pursue a relationship when he returns"

"You have to do what you feel is right for you, but he probably just wants to know that you will not be dealing with anyone else while he is so far away. It sounds like he just does not want to take a chance on losing you. Honestly, that is what you should want from a man, someone who will do anything to keep you."

"When you met Kevin, how did you know he was the one?" I asked.

"Kevin said the moment that he met me he knew that I was the one. It took me a little longer, probably about 6 months or so. You can't put a time limit on it you have to just trust your heart. This man seems to be genuinely interested in you, I must say" She said convincingly.

"I will consider what you have said but I don't know something just seems a little off about this."

We went on about our day. I had to see a client which required me to leave the office.

Once I had completed my work with my client it was time for me to get off, so I headed back to the house. I worked in a small town about 40 minutes from home, so it typically made for a good ride home. I had time to think about my day and just process some decisions that I needed to make. I normally would turn my music on and listen songs. When I am in the car by myself, I can sing without judgment not that I couldn't sing. Well, I can carry a tune, I didn't sound horrible, but I did not really like to sing in front of people. It was the time that I could just open up and let it all out. Music was such a release for me. There were always songs that I could related to and made me think of my current or past situations. So, there I was belting out *Love takes time* by Mariah Carey, riding down the road with the song on repeat. I had to pick my daughter up from my parent's house and I thought it would be a fine time to speak with my mother about everything that was going on with Jaiden and me.

IT'S GETTING SERIOUS

I arrived at my mom and dad's house. When I arrived at the door, my daughter, Alexis greeted me at the door "Mommy, Mommy" she screamed as she ran and gave me a hug. She always greeted me with the biggest smile. She made my heart skip a beat. "Hey baby, how was your day at school?"

"Good" she replied

"Did you learn lots of new things today?"

"Yup."

"Will you tell me all about it when we get home?"

"Yes, mommy." she said smiling.

"Great, I want to talk with grandma about a few things, can you gather your things and wait for me in the living room and watch Dora until we are ready to go?

"Yes ma'am" she replied and ran down the hallway.

I watched her go down the hall and my mother turned to me and said, "is something wrong".

"No mom, I just wanted to get your advice on something" I had been very discreet about my dealings with Jaiden up until this point. She had no clue what has been going on between us. My mom sat down at the kitchen table with a look of concern "okay, what's going on?"

"Well, you remember the man that I met a little while back, Jaiden?"

"Yes, I remember you telling me about him, what about him?"

"Well we have been in constant communication now since we met a few months ago. He has been very nice to me, I like him."

"Well that's good, isn't it?"

"Yes, but he in Iraq now on deployment and he has been really trying to get me to be in a relationship with him."

"Okay and you don't want to be in a relationship with him?"

"I just think that it is awkward that he wants to be in a relationship this soon after meeting me and with him being deployed. I mean he is attractive, he is a single father and given my past experiences with Alexis' father, who is not in her life, I have a great deal of respect for that. He sent flowers to my job today which I thought was a lovely gesture and I am thankful to have someone taking that much of an interest in me. When we talk he asks about Alexis too, as though he is genuinely interested in her and you know that it is a big thing for me. If I am going to be in a relationship with someone, they have got to be willing to accept Alexis as their own just as I would accept their kids as my own. It's just that he began asking me to marry him at the end of our first date and ever since then he has been trying to get me to commit to him in some way. I don't have much experience with men, but this seems odd to me. You know that I have been fooled before and I don't want to ignore anymore red flags."

"You said he is in the army, right?"

"Yes"

"Well chile that's how those army men operate, its nothing to worry about, I don't think. If you like him and you want to see where things go just give him a chance. Army men are just the settling down type, so he may just want to settle down with you but that's not a bad thing. Just see where his head is at but be careful" she said as she looked down over her glasses.

My mother was the second person to tell me to just see where things go with him. I knew that we would be speaking tonight, and he would inevitably ask me to be his woman. Should I just give in and see where things would go? After all, he was a few thousand miles away what was the worst that could happen. He could very well be the man that I have been searching for.

"Thanks mom" I said as I gave her hug.

"You're welcome baby. You know I am ready to see you with someone that can make you happy. You deserve to be happy. You have so many good qualities, someone is bound to snatch you up and cherish you for who you are. Look at your father and I, we married three months after we met. Chile, he knows a good woman when he sees her, and he was in the army at the time" she said boastfully.

"Mom, I love you, thanks for listening. Where's dad?"

"Oh chile, he is still at work, you know he doesn't get in until around 8:30 and you're welcome baby".

I absolutely admired the relationship that my mom and dad shared. It was not perfect by no means, but they were committed to it and had been for over 30 years. I have seen them experience some ups and downs, but it was the commitment that has stuck with me all these years. It was the commitment that I was looking for when I committed to Kareem, but he fell short. I wanted to have a man who would ride with me through thick and thin, in good times and bad and in sickness and in health. *Was it possible that I had that type of commitment in Jaiden? Could I be pushing that type of commitment away?* I began to wonder if I should give in to Jaiden's request after all, I was already committed to him simply because that is just the type of woman that I am. I can only talk and get to know one potential mate at a time. I was not getting ready to begin seeing anyone else, so what was holding me back?

I was up all-night thinking about whether I should give in to Jaiden. I didn't get a wink of sleep. I knew that he would be calling soon and if our conversation started off like all our other conversations, he would be asking me to be his woman. I could either continue to say no and come up with excuses why we should just remain friends or I could give in and say yes and see where things go from there. Saying yes would not change anything because we were already behaving as though we were in a relationship. He said that he was not entertaining other women and I was certainly not entertaining other men. I had men that hit on me all the time, but I was only interested in Jaiden and I made that abundantly obvious.

It was going on 1:00am and my phone had yet to ring. I began to get worried. *Did I push him away? Is something wrong?* I knew that he was in hostile territory where he was deployed, could something have gone wrong? Every minute that passed increased the anxiety. I didn't know what to think. Every day since he has been deployed I had received a phone call from him between 11:30 pm and 12:30 am like clockwork. I began to get chill bumps. I had no way to contact him because he always called from a calling card. I was left to wait for his phone call and it was agonizing. Finally, at about 3:00 am I received a call from an unknown number.

"Hello" I said anxiously.

"Alyssa, hey I'm sorry it took me so long to call you. We had an incident this morning and we were on lockdown. I called you as soon as I could get to the phone".

"An incident? What happened?"

"Our base came under fire, it was crazy"

"What? Oh my God are you okay?"

"Yes, I am fine. It's pretty dangerous here"

Suddenly it hit me that if something happened to him, I would be devastated. I obviously had feelings for him and I knew that he had some strong feelings for me.

"Jaiden, I have been thinking about what you said about us being in a committed relationship. I want to see where things would go between us."

"You do? Are you sure? Oh, my goodness this is a perfect ending to an eventful day." He said with excitement.

"I am sure, I realize that you are extremely important to me and I am not interested in being with anyone else."

"Neither am I Alyssa, I have known since the moment I met you that you were the one, it's about time that you gave me an opportunity to prove to you that I am the one for you too."

I had hoped that I was making the right decision. I certainly had my hesitations given my past experiences. Kareem had come in and swept me off my feet but turned out to be my worst nightmare and I vowed that I would never allow that story to replay.

From that point, our relationship continued to blossom, I felt more and more attached to him. I wasn't sure where it would lead. He seemed to have it all together and his actions showed that he was totally into me. He had a good and stable career that he was dedicated to. He had a nice car. He didn't have a home, but I knew that it was not too hard for him to get one. The only reason that he didn't is because he was deployed which meant he was saving money. He was responsible enough to be a single parent. He spoke about his son and daughter quite often. I loved that, I respected that. He never gave me the impression that he was dishonest in anyway. He was attentive to my needs and he communicated well with me. We shared a great deal of common interests which we discovered through our conversations. There was no doubt that we shared feeling for one another. He was someone I could bring home to meet my parents. *What more could I ask for, right?* He was the perfect man for me. He was the complete opposite of what Kareem turned out to be. I decided that I would match his effort and start showing him that I appreciated him.

"How can I help you" said the cashier at the post office. She was very friendly and courteous.

"I would like to send this package to this address" I handed her a paper with an address that Jaiden had provided me with. She took the paper and keyed in the address, printed out a sticker and stuck it the package.

"That will be $35.45."

I was sending him a care package with all the things that he wanted that he could not purchase at his location. I put a few pictures, a couple of myself and one of Alexis and I and some CD's that I had made myself with some love songs that made me think of him. "Distance and time" by Alicia Keys was number one because it was exactly what we were experiencing. I also put a few bags of Swedish Fish, which was his favorite candy and some boxes of popcorn. I placed some toiletries such as shaving cream and razors, body wash and wash clothes in the box. This was the first time that I had ever sent something to a soldier overseas. I was new to the military lifestyle. I hoped that he would be happy with the items that I was sending him. It was a rather large box, so I did not blink when she told me the price that I would have to pay in order to send it.

"Here you are ma'am" as I handed her my debit card. She swiped the card and handed back to me along with the receipt.

"Here you go, you're all set, the package should arrive within 14-21 business days."

I get a package from him every other day or flowers with some of the sweetest messages. It has been a couple of months since I agreed to be in a relationship with him and he had been proving to me every day that I made the right decision. The gifts did not only extend to myself but to Alexis as well. For once, I felt like another man could love Alexis as his own. It was refreshing. I was glowing with a smile that beamed from ear to ear. I was on a natural high, that nothing or no one could bring me down from. My daughter was excited to have a father figure that took an interest in her and thought enough about her to buy her things and inquire about her. It was more than her biological father had done for her, so it was not as though she had a great deal of interaction with a father figure other than my father which was her grandfather. Though she had never met him she had spoken to him plenty of times during our video chats.

There was a time when Alexis was sick with the flu and I told him about how she was feeling. The following day he sent her a beautiful get-well arrangement. It was these types of gestures that had not only flattered me but had made me fall hard for this man. Alexis was excited too. I was on cloud nine and it was a feeling that I had never felt before. In the past, I had always been the one to put forth the effort with kind gestures and it had never been reciprocated. I was thrilled to have someone who was willing to match my efforts and I was ready to do so. *Was I falling in love with this man?* It was certainly possible. We spoke every day, we laughed together, we shared all our secrets, we both longed to be together. I knew that he would soon be coming homing for break and we were both counting down the days. I could not help but wonder what how we would interact when we were face to face versus being on the phone. Would I feel the same way about him? I knew that there was an attraction to him, but it had been so long since I had actually seen him face to face. I was excited but anxious to see if our face to face interaction would be as pleasurable as all our phone conversations. We had only shared a few dates before he left and while they were enjoyable, I was in a different frame of mind at that time. I was closed off to being in a relationship and now we were in a long-distance relationship. I was worried that it would be awkward when we met again.

He would be returning just in time for my friend's/co-workers wedding. I had asked her if it would be okay for him to attend and naturally she agreed that he could. I had to ask him if he would accompany me while he was home, but I never doubted that he would. I had so much to do to prepare for the wedding. I had to go and get fitted for my dress and I had to pick out some accessories. I decided to do everything on a weekend that my mom had Alexis and it was no telling when she would agree to keep her again on the weekend.

Once I completed all my errands, I went back to my parents' house to pick Alexis up. I walked in the door and was greeted by father. "Hey Alyssa, how have you been? Seems like I haven't seen you in forever. What's going on?"

"Nothing much, just had to run a few errands, figured since I was done I would go ahead and get Alexis to spend some time with her."

"Oh okay. That sounds good. Do you have any plans or are you just going with the flow?"

"I am just going with the flow. I am gonna see what she wants to do and go from there."

"Let me know what you decide, I may want to hang out with you all if that's okay." My dad loved to spend time with us. He was as big on family as I was. Perhaps, that is where I got it from.

"Okay I will".

"So, your mom tells me you have a new boyfriend, why haven't I heard about him? He looked at me a side eyed.

I shyly responded. "Well we were just seeing where things would go, and he is overseas now but I would love for you to meet him".

"Oh yeah, where is he?"

"He is in Iraq, he is a soldier in the army"

"Oh really!!!! An army man, huh? I thought you would never date an army man."

"I never thought that I would either Dad but he kind of came along dispelled all of those myths that I had heard about men in the Army. I really like Jaiden; our relationship may be getting serious."

My dad had a worried look on his face and I was not sure where it was coming from considering what I had just told him about how into Jaiden I really was. I valued my father's opinion, but he really did not express much of an opinion one way or the other. My father and I had a great relationship. We went to dinner occasionally, out to movies and we took a lot of family trips. Many people thought that it was odd for me to want to take trips with my parents at my age, but I valued family. I wanted to keep a close bond with my family, tomorrow isn't promised, and my parents are not going to live forever so I cherished every moment that I could spend with them. I spent more time with them than I spent with my friends because I was not into going to clubs and bars and my friends were. I certainly was not knocking them for it, it just wasn't my thing. For me the words 'family over everything' rang true.

Later that day, I decided that I would call Nicole and see if we could set up a playdate. She was going to be moving to Greensboro, NC soon and I wanted them to spend as much time together as possible. I knew that once she left, their interactions would be far and few between considering that it was hours away from where we were. Nicole and I were not friends like we were at one point, but she was someone that I considered family, because our kids were siblings. I let the past be the past and we moved forward for the sake of our children. We talked about how their father, Kareem, had abandoned our children, we talked about our future endeavors and we talked about our love lives. Nicole had met someone special and she was engaged to get married. She was moving to Greensboro, NC with her fiancé. She seemed so happy and I was happy for her. Even after the havoc she wreaked in my life, I still believe that she is a good person and she deserved to be happy.

HOMECOMING

The day has finally arrived when I would be going to pick Jaiden up from the airport. I had a wealth of emotions that I was going through, excitement and nervousness to name a couple. I felt the butterflies fluttering in my stomach, I thought our first time seeing one another face to face in such a long time going to be magical or a dud. I mean it was no way to really know for sure. I just had to wait and see how this would go. As I approached the location where I would pick him up, I took a deep breath and exhaled. It was the moment of truth and I was ready to face it head on.

I walked into the building and there were so many people there it was difficult to navigate. Considering this was my first time having to do something like this, I walked around looking clueless, looking for some direction. I stood there looking for him in his uniform and I didn't see him or anyone else with a uniform. I only saw sleuths of people holding balloons, flowers, welcome home posters, and pictures of their love ones. You could see the excitement in their eyes, but I did not feel that same excitement and I was not sure why. I just wanted to see him again and see how we connected. Someone came over the intercom and introduced the troops back on mainland and the crowd went wild clapping and the tears were flowing all around me. I watched as hundreds of troops stepped off a plane and walk into the building eagerly waiting to see Jaiden. Some of the loved ones would run toward their soldier with the kids in their hands and hug them like they sorely missed them. It was a beautiful sight to see all these families reunited, mothers and fathers back with their children, husbands and wives back with their spouses, boyfriends and girlfriends back with their significant others. For a moment I thought, *is this going to be me?*

Suddenly Jaiden appeared and when I saw him I ran to him and gave him a hug and kiss. We looked each other in the eyes and told one another how much we missed each other. We had a couple of minutes to catch up before another announcement came up for the troops to return to their command and for the loved ones to await the troops in a specific location. I could not help but notice this female soldier whose name read Lopez on her uniform. She was not with the troops who were coming in, but she looked as if she was waiting on someone too. For some reason she appeared to be eye-balling me instead. I gave Jaiden a hug and kiss and told him I would be waiting for him in the location in which they told us to wait. This woman appeared to be studying my every move but once they called the soldiers she just disappeared.

I walked out to the car and drove around to the location. I waited and waited for hours in that location and still no signs of him. Finally, I saw him appear and he went into a building with all his gear and signaled that he would be right back. I waited in the parking lot for about an hour longer. I was starving, this appeared to be an all-day event and frankly I was getting a little frustrated because I was not prepared for it. I did not want to take my frustration out on him though, after all we had not seen each other in months. He had disclosed that his favorite meal was steak and potatoes during our many phone conversations, so I had left a pot roast in the crock pot simmering with the potatoes and vegetables. I was not worried about the pot roast because it was slow cooking in the crockpot which only meant that it was going to be tender. I just knew that this would be the icing on the cake if he were in love with me before, after he had my cooking he would be head over heels in love with me. You know what they say, cooking is the way to a man's heart and I am a damn good cook if I do say so myself.

I had envisioned that once we got home that our evening would be magical like my first time with Kareem. Our physical attraction was not quite as strong as it was with Kareem and me. In a way, I thought that, it may be a good thing. I mean I certainly wanted that connection to be there, but I was willing to sacrifice some of that to have a man that would treat me the way I deserved to be treated. I felt that if he treated me well and we had some attraction that the rest would fall into place.

The aroma of home cooking hit us when we stepped out of the car in front of the house. As we got closer to the door the aroma intensified. "Oh my God, something smells delicious, smells like something good is cooking. I can't wait to find out what it is." Jaiden said as he rubbed his hands together in anticipation.

"Just a lil something I put together to make sure you had a nice welcome back."

"What is it? I know it is going to be good".

"I made a pot roast with potatoes and vegetables".

We walked in the door at the house and the it smelled as if we had walked into the best soul food restaurant in town. I knew that he would be hungry, and I was starving. "Would you like for me to fix your plate honey?"

"Yes, that would be nice." He dropped his gear on the living room floor and sat down at the table. I prepared his plate for him and let him sit down to eat a nice homecooked meal. We sat down at the candle lit table across from one another.

"Man, that was delicious. Beautiful, sweet and you can cook, oh yeah, you are a keeper." He laughed as he scrapped his plate clean with his fork. I got up and grabbed both of our plate and walked to the kitchen. "Let me show you around." I showed him every room in the house so that he would become familiar with the surroundings. Afterwards, he flopped down on the couch.

"Man, I'm tired and my belly is full." He said grinning like a Chester cat.

"Well, I have somewhat of a surprise for you. Stay here and just relax for a minute." I said to him as I handed him the remote control for the TV. I wanted him to be able to relax since he had been in transit to get back in the states for the last 48 hours. I walked back to the master bathroom and filled the garden tub with hot water and lit little lavender scented tealight candles all around the tub. I turned the music on softly playing a nice Kenny G Jazz CD. I went back up front to get him and he was still sitting on the couch watching TV.

"I ran you some bath water. I want you to sit and relax for a while". I sat the towel, washcloth and bar of soap on the side of the tub.

"Thank you, baby," he said with amazement. He was enthused that I had gone through such lengths to make him happy. He began to undress, and I walked out the room. We had not been intimate, and I wanted to give him his privacy. I didn't feel comfortable being in there while he bathed. He sat there in the tub for a few minutes and then I heard him call out my name. I walked into the bathroom "hey, did you call me?"

"Yes, I thought you would like to give me some company"

"Company? While you are in the tub?"

"This is a big tub, I think we can both fit in here." I thought, *this is not the way I had anticipated this going.* "Don't you want to take a shower bath too. Come on, I won't bite".

I felt uncomfortable. I declined and told him I was planning on taking a shower in the other bathroom while he was relaxing. He seemed a little disappointed, but I had a whole plan together and I intended to see it through. He would only be here for a few weeks and then he would be heading back to finish out his tour overseas. I wanted to make the best of our time and since I knew that the mental connection was there, I wanted to make sure the physical connection was there as well. I had hoped that I wasn't moving too fast but what woman wants to spend their lives with a man that they share no physical connection with, right?

I went into the bathroom and took a nice hot, steamy shower. I stepped out, dried myself off and pulled out some lingerie that I had purchased from Victoria Secret. It was plum colored cheeky bikini's and a matching push up bra. I pulled out the baby oil and rubbed down every inch of my body. I sprayed some 'light blue' perfume behind my ears, on my wrist and between my thighs. I looked in the mirror and ran my hands across my stomach and down my hips. I wanted to make sure he could see my curvy silhouette once he walked into the dimmed room. I put on some lip gloss, stretched my eyelashes out with some mascara and let my hair down. I had never really been big on wearing a ton of makeup. I heard the water draining in the tub and I started to hurry. I wanted to have the room set up with the candles and have everything in place when he walked out. I grabbed my floral robe which matched my bra and panties and rushed into the bedroom and lit the candles. I turned the lights off and the glow from the candles was the only light. I heard him coming to the door, so I stepped out for a moment. Once he walked out of the room with only a towel around him and turned the lights off in the bathroom, I walked in.

There I stood with a chilled bottle of champagne in one hand and two champagne flutes in the other hand. "Wow, you look amazing." He walked toward me with the towel draped around his waist. He didn't have a physique like Kareem, but he had an athletic build.

"Thank you" I said as I smiled.

He placed his hands on my hips as if he knew what was about to go down. He looked me in my eyes and said, "damn I missed you". He kissed my lips gently. I handed him a champagne glass and the bottle of champagne, so he could pop the cork. We sat on the bed and indulged. We conversed for hours as if we were catching up on all the lost time. You would think that we hadn't spoken every day the entire time he had been gone. I was thrilled to know that the first thing on his mind was not sex, but I was also thinking that he may not be attracted to me because he did not try anything with me. Here we both were laying in the bed half naked and the mood was set but he was not trying to make a move on me. *Am I going to have to make the first move?* We continued talking but I was becoming discouraged because there was no way that I was going to make the first move with him. I got up off the bed and he pulled me back. "where are you going?"

"I was getting ready to turn on lights."

"Turn the lights on for what? Come here let me whisper something in your ear."

I moved closer to him and he whispers in my ear. "You are the sexiest woman in the world and you are all mine. I'm the luckiest man alive." He began to nibble on my ear and if what he had said had not moved me, his lips against my skin certainly had. He had the sexiest full lips. He brushed his lips against my skin from my neck down to my breasts while undressing me with his hands. He released the towel from around his waist and placed his hand in between my legs. He whispered in my ear "I love you and I'm going to give you the world." I melted just with the sound of those words. His feelings for me were lucid through each stroke. Our bodies had joined together, and it was as if our souls had become one. Once we both reached our climax, He looked out at me with a huge grin on his face and said, "you are simply amazing". He rolled over and we fell asleep in each other's arms.

I woke up the next morning lying beside him. I laid there in the bed just thinking about the night before. I knew that it was not right for me to compare experiences, but I couldn't help it at this point. While I enjoyed the experience and it felt as though we had connected on a deeper level that night, I was not fully satisfied. The sex with Kareem and I was mind-blowing, intense, and we could go all night. Now, with Jaiden, it was good but there was no stamina to go all night and it lacked intensity. I am an understanding person, I knew that it had been a while for him, so I attributed that performance to that fact. I was somewhat disappointed because our first time did not meet my expectation by any stretch of the imagination, but I was still hopeful.

I had a million and one thoughts running through my head. He could be the one that I am going to spend my life with and I wandered if this would be the extent of our sex life. If so, how happy could I really be. No, sex is not everything, however, it could be a deal breaker if it was not satisfying but I would like to think that I was not that shallow. I do not care about sex. I care about getting treated well, the sexual aspect can be worked out I suppose. I walked into the kitchen and began cleaning the dishes that I had left in the sink the night before. Before long, I felt Jaiden walk up behind me. He placed his hands over my eyes as if to blindfold me and said "I have a surprise for you, you have to keep your eyes closed until I say open them"

"okay" I said as I giggled feeling the suspense.

He placed a necklace around my neck and since I could feel it, I started to get excited.

"Wait, don't open your eyes yet, I have one more surprise" he said.

"Okay" I replied with the biggest grin a woman could wear. It felt as though he left me standing there. I did not hear him anymore nor did I feel him behind me any longer. "Jaiden" I called out.

"Yes" he said as he turned me around. When I opened my eyes and he was down on one knee with a box in one hand. The shock I felt at that moment was indescribable, but I thought to myself *surely, he is not getting ready to propose to me.* In that moment, he says "Alyssa, will you be my wife?" I did not know how to respond. Was I even ready for such a big step? In that moment I thought about all the advice that I had been given about Jaiden. I thought about what my mother and father said and what my friend Vanessa told me about her current fiancé who she would be marrying in just a few days. I thought about how ready I was to give my heart to that special person for a lifetime and build that family unit. I thought about how eager Alexis was to have a father figure in her life since her biological father was not there and how this decision could ultimately impact her as well. I loved him, and I was ready for a commitment, so I answered after a long pause "Yes I will be your wife, Jaiden!".

He was ecstatic, he placed the ring on my ring finger. I glanced at the ring intently on my finger. I loved the way it looked to have an engagement ring on my finger. I forgot all about our first time not that it was all that memorable, but I felt like any issues that may arise we could get through it. This was a new chapter for me. After all that I had been through with Kareem and I was looking forward to it.

It was time to break the exciting news to my parents and I felt that it was time for him to meet my daughter in person. If we're going to get married, I need to be sure that he was good fit for her as well. I also wanted to make sure that I met his son. We began to make plans to meet his son and his mother in Philadelphia and of course it was easy to plan for him to meet my daughter. I was happy. I think I was happier to rebuild my family than I was about spending my life with Jaiden. Plain and simple, I was happy to be getting married. I met with my parents and they were happy for me as well. Jaiden had left quite an impression on them and my daughter loved him. It was refreshing to see her run through the door and straight to him to give him a hug when I picked her up from school. After our trip to Philly, I kept in contact with his son and mother and they both seemed to love me too. It was shaping up to be a good fit for everyone. Jaiden and I spent every moment of that three weeks together, that is when I was not working. We had become inseparable. We got along well. He treated me great. I had no complaints. I had no idea what was in store for the future, but it seemed like a welcome change.

We stayed engaged for a year while we planned the wedding. Six months of that he was overseas then we moved in together as a family we he returned. Everything was beautiful, no arguments and we did most everything together as a family. Everyone got along well. I couldn't ask for a better outcome. My wedding day was quickly approaching. Jaiden had done most of the planning and handled the bulk of the expenses. My parents offered to absorb some of the expenses, but Jaiden was a proud man and he wanted the day to go as he planned so he would not allow them to pay a dime. The only expense that I took care of was my wedding dress and the cake. I had picked out a beautiful gown that looked like a something from a fairytale. At that time, that is what my life resembled, a fairytale. Little did I know my life was about to take an unexpected turn for the worse.

VOWS

I was standing at the doors of the church looking into the glass window admiring the beautiful decorations and all the guest who had come to share this beautiful occasion. I was holding my father's arm as we waited to walk down the aisle. I was filled with emotions, but I couldn't figure out why one of them was sadness. This was supposed to be a joyous occasion, but I was ready to cry. I think that subconsciously, I was sensing that something was getting ready to go awry. I should have listened to all the red flags that were waving high in my head, but I instead chose to mute them out.

The music cued, and my father and I entered through the doors. I could see Jaiden standing there waiting for me at the altar. He was dressed in his dress blues army uniform, looking very handsome. I could see the smiles of the guests as we walked down the aisle. What should have been a couple minutes to get down the aisle felt like an eternity. The closer I got the more anxious I became and the sadder I got. I approached, and the pastor began to officiate the wedding. The pastor announces, "who gives this woman to be wed?"

"Her mother and I do" said my father smiling with pride.

The pastor continued with a prayer and asked if we had written our own vows. I had not but to my surprise Jaiden had.

"Yes, I do" he said aloud.

"Okay go ahead, young man"

He walked toward Alexis and knelt down on one knee. "Alexis, even though I have not been there for your entire life it feels like I have been your father since you were born. If I could go back in time to change that fact I would but since I can't I want, you to know that I will be the father that you deserve until the end of time. I promise to protect you from harm, shield you from the harsh realities of this world, listen when you need a shoulder to lean on and give you guidance when it is needed. I take you to be my daughter forever more. Do you take me to be your father, and your protector for now and forever more?"

"Yes" she cried out as tears streamed down her face. She was genuinely touched by the gesture and in that moment she had developed an unmatched level of respect for him.

He gave her a hug. Alexis was sobbing uncontrollably. I was in tears. Hell, the whole church was in tears. There was not a dry eye in the house. My parents were glowing with excitement and a look of relief settled over their faces as they wiped the tears away. I felt the relief too, the fears and sadness that I was facing as I entered the church had faded just as quickly as they came on. It was one of the sweetest gestures that I had ever experienced, and Jaiden turned to me and held both of my hands. "Okay, it's your turn Alyssa" he said as he gently wiped the tears from my face.

"From the moment I met you, I knew that you would be my wife. You gave me a hard time at first, but I was so glad when you came around. You became my best friend, my confident, my shoulder to lean on, my everything. You deserve to be loved deeply and I want to give that love to you. I promise to do everything in my power to be the man that you want and need all the days of our lives. I promise to respect your wishes, support your dreams and provide for you and our family. I promise to love you through thick and thin, in sickness and in health, for better or worse, til death do us part. I, Jaiden take you Alyssa to be my lawfully wedded wife for now and forever more. Do you Alyssa take me Jaiden, to be your husband til death do us part?"

"I do."

The pastor intervened "This is my part, Jaiden. You may now kiss the bride"

This is the part when everything started to go downhill. Jaiden moved in to kiss me and took a deep breath. I felt the atmosphere change as we walked out of the church hand in hand. We stepped into the limo and suddenly that feeling of dread came over me again. I looked at Jaiden and watched him breathe what appeared to be a sigh of relief. It was almost as if he had flipped a switch and I felt his energy change.

That night we sat in the hotel and what was supposed to be a celebration of our new union turned into a pity party. I was crying hysterically and the only explanation I could offer is that I just had a bad feeling. I felt that things would end badly between us. I felt like I had made a mistake. It was such a strong and overwhelming feeling. I was supposed to be happy, but I wasn't. I guess looking back, I could have called it a premonition. At this point, all I could do is be hopeful that I had made the right decision and that all the vows that he made before God, he intended to honor.

The following week we had planned to take the kids to Disney world to celebrate our new family. I think it became evident to everyone that something was off while on this trip. I had been ill, but I had attributed my illness to stress. I noticed right away that the way he treated his son was much different than I was used to. He was short with him, not as compassionate as he once was and at some points he was violent. He would just punch him in the chest because he did not respond to a question the way that he thought that he should. He became short with me. The atmosphere became ice cold in our home. But, I vowed to stick with him through better or worse and there was no way I was going to just give up on my family.

A couple months later, I decided that it was time for me to take a pregnancy test. I had been sick for too long, missed my cycle, it was a familiar feeling. Positive. That plus sign that popped up caused me to go through a wealth of emotions. I wandered if he would be happy when I told him, would this lighten the mood or intensify the mood at the house. We were married, and we had to get through this. I went to the store and purchased a hallmark card and wrote a cute note in it expressing how much I loved him. I enclosed the pregnancy test in the card and walked into the room to hand it to him He opened the envelop and looked up at me, eyes wide. I didn't know if he was going to pass out from the shock, if he was pissed, or if he was just that happy. "You're pregnant?"

"Yes, are you happy?"

"I am ecstatic. I have been waiting for this day." He reached out and squeezed me tightly.

"I wasn't sure if you would be happy, you have been on edge lately."

"I know baby, I have just had so much going on with work. I have to get up out this company I'm in, but I can't wait to see our little bundle of joy. I want a little girl. How far along are you? Do you know?"

"I'm guessing I'm about 3 months. I have suspected for a while, but I think I was too scared to find out." Jaiden had no idea about the miscarriage I had suffered when I was with Kareem. That was something I did not talk about to anyone because it brought up old memories. I just did not want to find out until I thought that I was past the first trimester. Things started to improve in the house. Jaiden seemed happier and more playful with the kids.

When I was about 7 months pregnant Jaiden came to me and told me that he had signed up to take a 12-week course that would be split up into two sections. One would be a 6-week section that he would leave for now and the other six-week section was scheduled for 2 days after my due date. *What if I were to have the baby late, would he be there?* When he left for the first class, we kept in constant contact.

One early morning however, while lying in bed, tossing and turning because my belly was so big that I couldn't get comfortable. My phone rings at 4:44 am and Jaiden's name comes up on my caller ID. *Why would he be calling me at this hour?* He never called me this early. *Was something wrong?*

"Hello" I said anxiously.

"Hello---" I continued. I could hear a swooshing noise and I could faintly hear his voice in the background.

"Jaiden are you there?" I then heard a female voice faintly in the background. *Who the hell is this woman he talking to at 4:44 in the morning?* I heard some ambiguous conversation between him and another woman. I sat up in my bed, now trying to listen intently. My ear glued to the phone, pressing it into my ear so that I could try to make out some of this conversation. Unfortunately, I could not make out a word, but it was enough for me to have a conversation with him about who the hell he was talking to. I hung the phone up and dialed him back. He answered "Hello."

"Good morning" I said sarcastically

"Good morning, what's up?"

"You tell me, you called me first"

"No, babe you just called me, I'm on my way to PT"

I had to think of something quick to get him to fess up even though I didn't hear the conversation clearly. "Well you called me, I guess by accident and I stayed on the phone for a while. You were with a woman talking about what y'all did last night....so what was that about?"

I got a dead silence on the other end. "Yeah you outed yourself. Go ahead and go to your PT."

-Click

He called and called back to back, and I didn't answer. This man was all the way in another state and at the very least he was entertaining another woman. The fact that I didn't know the extent of their dealings was taking a toll on me. My mind was like a whirlwind wondering if he had done anything with this mysterious woman. What was worse is that I didn't see any of this coming. I sat in my bed and cried. Here I was crying again in anguish over the actions of the man in my life. I didn't know what to think. I didn't want to jump to conclusions. After all it was just a conversation that I had overheard. It was not as though I could make out anything that was said but something inside me said that it was more than just a friendly conversation. He was set to come home that following day to spend the weekend. I didn't know how I was going to interact with him knowing that while I was at home pregnant and taking care of two children that he was entertaining another female. He tried to call me several times, but I just went dark on him and never returned his calls. I had nothing to say to him. I went through my day as usual so busy with the kids that I barely had time to think about what happened earlier.

The next day, I started to get nervous about his arrival. I did not know what I would do or say when I saw him. *Am I going to throw something at him? Am I going to cuss him out? Am I going to be that rational person who allows him to explain?* He walked into the door around 4'oclock looking like a little puppy dog with his tail tucked between his legs. His eyes were lowered, there was a look of dread that ran across his face. I could only imagine that he did not know what to expect from me no more than I knew how I would react when I was able to confront him face to face. All I could do was look at him, study his movements, his expressions just to gauge what the situation could have been. He greeted the kids and they ran to him and gave him a big hug. They both shouted, "We missed you Dad!" The happiness that my daughter displayed made forget all about what happened. I appreciated him for stepping up to take care of a child that did not biologically belong to him. The fact that she loved him to made it hard for me to take up any issues with him and for that reason, I just wanted to kiss and make up. I also wanted a logical explanation for what I did hear. I was hoping he would tell me something like he just had a friendly dinner with her and some other friends the night before and beg me not to be upset.

I allowed him to spend some time with the kids, they wanted to be right up under him. I decided that it was best for me to wait until the kids were in bed to address the elephant in the room. I stayed in the kitchen cooking. I made stuffed chicken breasts, creamed spinach and homemade mashed potatoes. I baked a cake called 'Hummingbird Cake', it was kind of like a banana bread cake with pineapples and a homemade Coconut Lime cream cheese frosting.

You see, when I have something brewing in my mind, I cook elaborate meals and bake to take my mind off it. When the food is done everyone seems to be happy. My cooking seems to have that effect on people but I'm not bragging.

We all sat down at the table and enjoyed the food that I had prepared. Everyone scrapped their plates clean, all you could hear was the sound of the forks scrapping against an empty plate. My step-son may as well of licked the plate. "Can I have some more, Mom?" he said with excitement. He was a growing boy and I wouldn't dare deny him seconds with that in mind. "Of course, you can." I was delighted that he enjoyed my cooking enough to ask for seconds. I got up from the table and began to clean the kitchen and Alexis got up and said she was done with her food. I instructed her to go take a bath and get ready for bed. I walked to the back to run her bath water.

I walked back to the kitchen and continued cleaning. By this time, both the kids had gone their separate ways to prepare for bed. Jaiden was sitting at the table still shoving the last of his food around the plate. Clearly, he had something on his mind that he wanted to get off. I refused to be the one to initiate the conversation, after all, he did not seem to have any issues making conversation as evidenced by the lengthy conversation he was having with that woman first thing in the morning.

I was still a little salty about the incident, but I was trying not to overreact. It was difficult because of things that I suffered in my past, but I thought I was doing well all things considered. I stood over the sink washing dishes, we had not uttered a word to one another since he walked through the door. Jaiden walked up behind me and wrapped his arms around me. I rolled my eyes and sighed, although he could not see me rolling my eyes, I'm sure he felt it. He delicately kissed me on my shoulder, his lips brushed against my skin and he whispered softly in my ear "I'm sorry".

I turned toward him to look him in the eyes "I'm sorry for wh---?" I started to ask but before I get the words out he put his finger to my lips to hush me. He took me by my hand and led me to the bedroom. *Maybe he wants some privacy so that he can explain to me why he is apologizing.* I walked back with him hesitantly where he sat me down on the edge of the bed. He got down on his knees and knelt before me and placed his head in my lap. I was still slightly bewildered because he had not said anything but "I'm sorry". He laid there in my lap for a few minutes locking his arms around me as if it was the last time he would ever hold me. He lifted my dress and began to kiss me between my thighs. He pulled the dress over my head and began to kiss my growing belly. The stretch marks looked like a road map across my belly and hips, but he embraced every single line. As badly as I wanted to be mad at him, in that moment, my hormones had a mind of their own and I was welcoming his actions. That night, he made love to me in a way that I had never experienced with him. It was passionate, exciting yet tender, sensual and extraordinary. When I climaxed, I felt a tear roll down my cheek. These were not tears of sadness, these were tears of joy. This had been one of the best sexual encounters that we had ever had. We had reached new heights and he made me feel things that I had never experienced with him. It was as if he was making love to me for the last time.

He sat on the edge of the bed putting his clothes back on. He still looked like he had lost his best friend and by this time, I was thinking that he would be grinning from ear to ear. He stood up and looked at me as I laid in the bed and he said it again "I'm sorry".

"You're sorry for what Jaiden? If there is something that you want to tell me just spit it out."

"Well I----I---I don't know how to say this."

"You better think fast Jaiden"

"I cheated on you and I feel really bad about it."

My mouth dropped, and I sat upright in the bed and swung my legs to the side to stand up. "What did you just say?" I was hoping that my ears were deceiving me.

"I cheated on you Alyssa and I know I ain't shit for that".

I jumped up off the bed and grabbed my clothes to get dressed. "You cheated on me while I was pregnant with your child and then you came home and made love to me like nothing happened? You son of a bitch. How could you do this to me and your unborn child? How could you do this to your family?" Here was another red flag I had chosen to ignore. I mean they were waving high when I received that butt dial phone call. Even though I couldn't make out what was said, it should have held more weight with me.

I ran out the door and jumped in my car. I sped off out of the driveway. I was furious but most of all I was hurt. Cheating on your pregnant wife is by far the worst thing you could quite possibly do to a woman. It had me questioning myself like *what the hell was I not doing to make him feel like he needed to cheat on me while I was pregnant? How long had this been going on?* I had a million and one questions swirling in my head but there was nothing that he could say to me at this point that would make any sense.

I was racing down the road, going about 65 in a 45 MPH zone, swerving in and out of lanes. I looked in my rearview and there he was following me, flashing his lights on me to pullover. The rational side of me thought that it was best to pull over not for him but for my unborn child. I needed to be safe and this was not a safe situation. I pulled over, my face flooded with tears. *Why does this keep happening to me? What have I done to deserve this treatment?* I sat in my car and he walked up to the driver's side window. He tapped on the glass and I just looked at him. Did I really want to hear what he had to say about this? What could his explanation quite possibly be? Why did he seem to be so concerned when didn't have that same concern when he was laid up with another woman while I was at home not only taking care of our children but carrying our unborn child as well? I looked up at him through the tinted windows wondering if he could see how distraught I was. I wiped the tears away from my face and pulled myself together. I rolled the window down "What Jaiden?"

"Listen, you have to believe me when I say that I never wanted to hurt you. You are a good woman and wife. I messed up, but I don't want to lose you and my family. Think about the kids." He knew that was my weakness, my family has always been my top priority.

"Think about the kids?" I said boldly. "Were you thinking about the kids when you were laid up with some woman? Huh? Were you?" I began to roll my window back up, blocking him out. I couldn't stand the sight of him at this point. I realized that this was the beginning of the end. *How do you recover from something like this and is it even worth trying to?* I had a lot to contend with, but I wasn't going to get anywhere sitting in the parking lot crying my eyes out.

I had to stifle my emotions quickly. I also had to think about the stress that I was putting on my unborn baby. You know when you are carrying a child, that child can feel everything that you are going through. I had already lost one baby which I believe that I lost because of the stress that I was going through with Kareem but those were just my thoughts of course. There was no conclusive medical proof that the miscarriage I had was a result of stress. It made me sad to think about my unborn child feeling the way that I was feeling in that moment. I had to snap out of it and put my big girl panties on. My kids needed me, and I needed to be the strong woman that I know that I could be, to deal with this. Jaiden just stood there looking into the window as he stood in the Wendy's parking lot that we had pulled into. I put my car in drive and pulled off without as much as a warning. If my better judgment would not have not have stopped me, I would have vectored my vehicle and rolled over his feet, but I refrained. I looked in my rearview to see a reflection of him watching me drive away.

DE'JA VU

I calmed down because I realized that driving erratically through town would not benefit anyone and it could ultimately be dangerous. I rode around for hours just thinking about what he had done, the damage that he has now caused. I thought about his audacity to tell me to my face and then I thought well at least he told me and he didn't lie about it. He could have been like Kareem and hid it for years. He could have had another girlfriend right under my nose and even gotten another woman pregnant right under my nose, but he was being honest about his mistakes. I tried to keep that in mind, of course it didn't make me feel any better. *Is this what I should expect from all men?* I began to wonder. If so, should I now forgive him for his misdeeds, after all, I vowed to stick with him through better and worse, through thick and thin until death do us part. *At what point do you neglect the vows that you make before God?* If I decided to leave him, how would this affect our children? All these tough questions and I had no answers. All I had was a broken heart. I was hurt deep down to my core.

I decided that I would not be the only one to face tough questions. I had done nothing to be under scrutiny. I pulled into the driveway and looked at the house that we shared. It seemed so dark and gloomy. I walked into the house and into the bedroom where he was sitting at the edge of the bed with his hands clasped and his head bowed. He looked up, "Alyssa, you're back! I was so worried about you. I have been calling you and it goes straight to voicemail."

"Yeah, I turned my phone off. I just needed some peace and quiet."

"Alyssa, I know you are pissed and you have every right to be. I don't know what I was thinking. You didn't deserve this. I feel terrible."

"You should feel terrible, imagine how I feel." He reached his hand out to caress my arm and I moved back.

"Don't touch me. You can sleep on the couch tonight. I'm really not interested in laying in the same bed with you. But before you go, I have a few questions. Maybe I want the answers and maybe I don't, but I am going to ask them anyway. These are things that I need to know in order to move on."

"Okay".

"You need to be completely honest because at this point I will find out the truth."

"Okay". He crossed his arms and waited for the incoming fire that I was about to send his way.

"First of all, did you wear a condom with this woman?"

"Yes of course I did, come on now. Do you think that I would put your and the baby's health at risk?" I rolled my eyes at the absurdity in that question.

"Was this some random woman?"

I could see that he was getting a little anxious with my line of questioning and I was a little nervous because I did not know what his response would be. "No, she is a friend of mine from work. Do we really need to get into all that?"

"Yes, What's her name?"

"Her name is Jovana, but that really isn't important is it?"

I didn't know what was worse, the fact that this was someone that he considered to be a "friend" or the fact that he was trying to evade the subject. "It's your fault these questions are being asked in the first place. If you want me to get past this, I need answers plain and simple. So, is this the first time?

He hesitated "Yes".

I was not convinced at his answer "Let me see your phone." I never went through his phone because there was never a doubt in my mind about his fidelity.

"No!" he quickly responded.

"No? You are going to come home with a confession like that, expect me to believe you and then tell me no. What the hell do you have to hide? You know what I'm not doing this." I walked out the room and stepped out on the back porch. This man can't be serious to have the audacity to tell me no to such an innocent request but now my wheels were turning. *What did he have to hide?*

Jaiden and I didn't talk for weeks after that other than the typical "hey how was your day" but only in front of the kids. He would often try to talk about how I was doing with the pregnancy, but he got nothing much from me in return. I was still highly inflamed about his secrecy and the trust that I once had for him was out the door. My mom always told me if you don't have trust in a relationship that you don't have anything at all. So, it would seem, we did not have anything at all. As the time neared for me to have the baby, which we learned was another baby girl, I began to feel more drawn to resolving the issues within our marriage. Maybe it was the jolting kicks in my belly that made realize that there was a little life growing inside of me that we had both created and she would be here soon. Once I hit 8 months, I knew that it was time to start coming up with names and planning for her arrival. We needed to be on one accord, in order to ensure things, go smoothly for all involved.

Marriage is hard work and I have never been one to give up on anything or anyone that I loved. I certainly was not going to give up on my family. We needed some help though because even with all my experience with families and counseling, I had no idea how to fix this. Divorce seemed like a tough pill to swallow not just for me but for the kids. I proposed the idea of marriage counseling to him and he agreed without hesitation. He said he wanted to work on our marriage and our family too. We began making calls and finally found someone who would see us shortly after the baby was set to be born.

The atmosphere in the house was callous. We were sleeping in separate rooms and our conversation was short, limited to the kids. For all practical purposes, we had become roommates. The children were starting to notice the distance and they started asking questions, questions I didn't know how to answer. I tried to avoid them at all cost watering them down with trips to the ice cream parlor and visits to Chuck E. Cheese. I was eagerly awaiting the birth of my daughter and the opportunity to get some help rebuilding our marriage for the sake of our children.

On May 18, 2011, we welcomed a beautiful, healthy baby girl and named her Aniya Janaé. Jaiden left to go for his second part of class the day after Aniya was born. He literally watched her come into the world and left the hospital to pack so that he could leave early in the morning. She was born at 8:52 pm and he was gone by midnight. He would have missed the whole thing if she had of come any later. His absence was extremely nerve racking. Especially, considering the last time he went to class, he came home and told me that he had cheated. I hardly had enough time to really worry about it though with the extra duties that having a newborn brings. I had help from my mother, but the only thing Jaiden could offer me was a phone call. The life of a military wife had its challenges and since this is what I had signed up for, I had to deal with it. The weeks seemed to go fast. Aniya was growing quickly. I felt as though Jaiden was missing a great deal already. I mean, even though she was only a couple of weeks old, he had already missed the vast majority of her life. Not to mention, he didn't have to deal with the late-night feedings, the dirty diapers, and the crying spells where you felt helpless because you had no idea why she was crying.

His absence gave me time to think about our situation without having to see him. It gave me time to decide if I was willing to forgive him for his indiscretions without being guilted into considering everyone else's needs but my own. However, the reality was that my purview was my family and keeping it together. I could not help but to consider the kids while making this decision. The concept of divorce was looming in my head like a dark cloud. There were some parts of me that were hopeful that we could get through for the sake of our family and other parts that were saying 'to hell with this, I deserve better'.

Jaiden arrived home as scheduled and the ice set in once again. It was cold, lonely and distant. I couldn't believe that this is what we had been reduced to, but it was in fact my truth. We both uttered a single "hi" and he went into his 'mancave'. This time he didn't even give the kids a proper greeting or any of his time. I could see the look of disappoint that befell upon their faces. Neither knew what to make of the distance that had been created but they both knew that something was awry. I attempted to take their minds off it by offering to go see a movie and giving dad sometime to unwind from his long trip. It seemed to work for the moment, but I knew if this continued so would their inquisition.

The following day, we had our first appointment with the marriage counselor. We rode in separate vehicles but arrived at about the same time. We walked inside the office and it was very welcoming and calming. There was a little machine that was playing the sound of the ocean. The sound of the ocean always makes me feel serene. We checked in with the secretary in the front office and waited for our names to be called. After waiting for just a few minutes our names were called by a man who had just walked out of his office "Jaiden and Alyssa Williams". We both jumped up and walked toward the gentleman. He reached his hand out to shake Jaiden's hand and then mine while saying "Hi my name is Charles Stanton, I am going to be working with you today, it's a pleasure to meet you both." He extended his hand pointing in the direction of his office and said, "Come on in, make yourselves comfortable."

We sat down on the couch, Jaiden on one end and me on the other. Immediately, Mr. Stanton noticed the distance, but he refrained from commenting. "So, what brings you two in today?"

We both waited for the other to speak but neither of us said a word. Finally, I said "Well Mr. Stanton, we are not doing so well in our marriage. We don't communicate and there has been some infidelity. One minute we were great and the next our marriage was falling apart piece by piece".

Jaiden just sat there in silence as if he was convicted by the statement.

"Infidelity huh? It says here that you have been married almost 2 years is this correct? Mr. Stanton asked.

"Yes sir, that is correct." I replied

"And when did this infidelity begin?

"I learned of it while I was about 7 months pregnant with our daughter Aniya". I replied as I put my head down in shame.

"That must have been devastating for you Alyssa". He said with concern.

"It was Mr. Stanton. I felt inadequate and unloved and after that he refused to show me his phone as if he had something to hide. He had the nerve to come home and tell me about it like it was nothing. I mean I appreciate his honesty, but I was I would have appreciated his loyalty more. Now, I just feel like I can't trust him. He hasn't done one single thing to try and rebuild that trust. We don't even talk!"

"Well, Jaiden----do you mind if I call you Jaiden or would you prefer Mr. Williams?

"Jaiden is fine sir."

"You can call me Chuck. He said as he cleared his throat. "So, Jaiden how does it make you feel to hear what your wife is saying?" He asked politely.

"Well----Chuck, I hate that I hurt her in that way. I don't know why I did what I did but I feel awful about it. She has basically shut me out and I have a hard time dealing with rejection. I don't want to lose my family, but I don't know how we are going to come back from this and it's all my fault."

I sat there and stared at Chuck to see what his response was. I was reading his body language to see what his mouth wanted to say but perhaps he couldn't in this setting.

"There seems to be a lot of damage done by these actions." Chuck said stating the obvious.

I shook my head in agreement. My leg was bouncing away because the fury was building up in me like it had just happened all over again.

Chuck recited the principles of marriage and we listened to his spill for the remainder of the session. It was our first session, so I did not expect to accomplish a whole lot but by the end of the session, I was feeling more distant than I did when we walked in. Jaiden had not said too much while we there. It was as if he did not want the help. He should have been pleading for my forgiveness but instead he was there like a lump on a log.

"I would like to see each of back individually so that we can effectively move forward together. Jaiden, I would like to see you first. Can you come in next week and Alyssa I will see you the following week? How do Wednesday's work for you?" He said as he looked over his glasses while simultaneously writing notes from our session.

"Wednesday is fine for me in the evening" Jaiden reported.

"Wednesday works for me as well." I said.

"Great I have you both scheduled for 5 pm. Jaiden you will be next week and Alyssa you will be the week after that."

We both agreed and headed out of the office. I walked to my car and he walked to his and we never said a word to one another. I hated feeling isolated. People should not feel that way when they are married. I tried to suck it up and I decided to head to the mall just to take my mind off everything. My mom had the kids and it was a perfect time for me to get a little 'me time'.

CHANCE ENCOUNTER

As I was walking through the mall, I noticed a familiar face, Kareem. He didn't appear to see me as he was looking down at his phone. I didn't know whether to hide or to make sure that he saw me. It had been so long since I had seen him. I decided that I would make sure that he saw me. I walked up to him and said, "Hey there Kareem, long time no see."

He was so taken off guard that he dropped his phone. "Oh my God, Alyssa!" He reached out to give me a big hug and squeezed me tightly. He examined me up and down and left to right "Wow, you look amazing."

"Thank you, you're not looking too bad yourself."

"How's my baby girl doing?" He asked as he changed his tone from playful to serious.

"She is doing well, but why are you asking? You haven't attempted to be a part of her life in seven almost eight years." I said sarcastically. Honestly, I couldn't believe that I was standing there having this conversation with him. He deserved the silent treatment from me for the way things ended between us and how he has handled our daughter, not to mention his son whom he fathered with my best friend. When I saw him again, it was like I had forgotten about all our negative interactions and only remembered how in love with him I once was.

"Alyssa, I am truly sorry for the way things ended. I was so ashamed of myself. I beat myself up about it for a long time. I still do. I just thought that our daughter deserved a better father than I could be. I have done a lot of soul searching and I am in a much better place. I haven't had a drink in years. I went back to school and got my degree and I went on to finish graduate school. I have a stable career and I am just continuously trying to better myself. I work with families now, you know I always wanted to help people. I think about you often and I often wonder what Alexis looks like now" he proclaimed.

"That's great Kareem!" I said proudly. It's like he had named all the things that I took issue with when we were together, and I was wishing would change.

He looked down at my hand and saw my wedding ring. "Wow, so you are married now?"

"Yeah, I got married almost 2 years ago."

"Okay" he said as if he was disappointed. "How are things going?"

I looked down in shame and said, "we are having some issues right now". The words came out of mouth and I immediately wanted to recant. *Why on earth would I need to share that type of information with him?* I could see him get a little frazzled.

"What do you mean problems? He is not mistreating you, is

he?" he inquired.

"Do you mean like you mistreated me Kareem?" I asked with my head tilted to the side and a smirk on my face.

"I walked right into that one, didn't I?"

"Yes, you sure did!"

"Okay, I won't pry but if you ever need anything don't hesitate to call me. I would love to see Alexis if I could. I do want to be a part of her life. I know I've missed a lot and I cannot make up for that, but I am her father and I want to be a father to her. I know it's a lot to ask and consider but please give it some thought before you say No" he pleaded as he handed me business card with his name and number on it. The business card had his name on it with the title Licensed Marriage and Family Counselor and his address and number. I placed the card in my wallet.

I couldn't even be mad with him anymore. There was nothing disingenuous about his confessions. He seemed like he had changed and grown quite a bit from the last time we spoke. He was Alexis' father and he had a right to be a father to her, but it was a lot to consider. I was certainly not the type of woman to keep my child away from her father. Although it would be very confusing for her, she had a right to see him. She knew that Jaiden wasn't her biological father however, he was the only father she had ever known. The truth of the matter was that Jaiden wasn't acting like much of father these days himself. Nor did I know how much longer this union was going to last. "Let me talk to my husband about this and see what his thoughts are. I really need to think about this myself."

Before I could bring him around Alexis, I had to know for sure that he was serious about being an active part of her life and that he was on the up and up. The only way to do this was to have more conversations with him and see where his head was really at. Years ago, I would not have even considered this conversation with him. But for some reason, I was open to this idea more than I thought I would ever be considering the vile things that he had done to me in the past. Ultimately it was not about me, it was about my daughter who was presently getting the cold shoulder from the man that vowed to be her father.

"Okay, well you have my number. Don't be a stranger." He said as he hit me with that million- dollar smile. My Goodness, he is looking as fine as ever. That body still chiseled and sculpted like a work of art now cloaked in suit and tie.

"I will be in touch, Kareem. Have a nice day." I said as I began to walk away.

"Oh, I will, now that I got a chance to see and talk to you." He declared as he gazed at me. I could feel his eyes piercing me as I walked away so I giggled to myself.

The wave of emotions that I was experiencing in that moment was unrelenting. I remembered how protective he was of me and how sweet he once was towards me. I recalled our sexual encounters and those toe curling experiences we shared. It was a feeling that I longed for but had yet to experience with my husband. Now that things have gone cold in my home, I was getting absolutely nothing from him. I remembered how much in love, I once was with Kareem. I felt those butterflies swarming in my stomach and a flash of heat, it took me by surprise. *What is this I am feeling?* I was feeling overwhelmed with emotion and thoughts of him were spinning in my head like a tornado. I decided that I had had enough of the mall and it was best for me to go home and collect my thoughts. The drive home only intensified my thoughts. Every song that played on the radio made me think of him and that smile he left me with. *Snap out of it Alyssa, you're a married woman now.* I thought to myself. Besides that, I would never consider entertaining someone who mentally and physically abused me, cheated on me and neglected my child.

I walked in the door expecting to open up some dialogue with Jaiden. I had this interaction with Kareem in the back of my mind but something in me said it was not the right time to share it with Jaiden. The first person I see is Alexis. "Hey baby, how was your day?" I say as I greet her.

"It was good mommy. I was student of the day today." She said smiling. "Where were you? I missed you. Dad seemed upset when he got us from grandma's."

"He did?" I inquired.

"Yeah he just got us and didn't talk to us. When we got home he went to his room and we didn't see him no more.

"I am sure he was just tired honey. Don't worry, he may have had a bad day at work today." I explained. I avoided the question about my whereabouts and sent her to take a bath so that she could get ready for the next day.

I walked to the 'man cave' and knocked on the door. "Come in" he answered.

"Hey, can we talk?" I asked politely.

"Sure"

I walked into the room and closed the door. The last thing I wanted was for the kids to overhear us if this turned into an argument. "Hey, listen I don't know how much more of this silence I can stand. The distance between us is difficult for everyone including the kids."

He just looked at me and gave me no response.

"I know we are going to counseling and I hope that it helps us, but I want us to be able to talk to one another at home as well." Still no response, just a look of despair and frustration. I decided that I had said enough without so much as a word in return from him and I walked out of the room. I had said my peace and he could either choose to work on it or he could allow things to drift even further apart. I don't really see how that was possible but....

Once I had gotten the kids settled for bed, I walked back into my bedroom, laid on the bed and thought about my chance encounter with Kareem. I was set to spend another lonely night in this artic climate I called home. Jaiden and I had been sleeping separate for a while now and the alienation had begun to interfere with my better judgement. I needed someone besides my parents to talk to and quite frankly, I didn't want to share what was going on with anyone else. Since, I had already let Kareem know that Jaiden and I were having problems, I decided to give him a call. Besides that, Kareem's said that he works with families now, he's a marriage counselor. *What is the harm?* I thought. I tip toed down the hall and walked out on the back porch. It was a beautiful starry night, there was a gentle breeze and the temperature was just right. I dialed his number peaking around the corner to make sure that Jaiden was not going to pop up on me, although I knew he wouldn't. Once he went into his 'man cave' he did not come out. He had it equipped with a fridge, microwave, loaded with snacks and there was a bathroom in there as well. He was usually so enthralled with his game that he wouldn't move away from the television.

"Hello" Kareem answered as if he had hurried to answer the phone.

"Hey, this is Alyssa" I said with hesitation while speaking in a soft tone.

"Oh! Hey Alyssa, what a pleasure hearing from you. I didn't think that I would."

"Why did you think that?" I asked.

"Well, given our history, I wasn't sure if you would have anything else to say to me, but I'm glad you did."

I jumped straight to the point. "You said that if I needed anything to call you".

"Yeah, what's going on? Are you ok?" He asked with concern.

"Yeah, I'm ok. It's just------it's jus— never mind" I said with uncertainty. "I shouldn't be discussing any of this with you, really but…."

"Are you and Alexis in danger?"

"No, No, it's nothing like that!"

"whew, ok" he said in a calming tone. "Well what is it Alyssa, I know you and I know you haven't decided this quickly about letting me see Alexis. It has to be something else."

"Welll---remember I told you that I was having problems with my husband?"

"Yes, of course."

"I need some advice from a male perspective." I remarked.

"Okay, I am happy to help." He said hesitantly.

"My husband and I have been sleeping in separate rooms and I don't know how to fix things with him. We have been distant ever since the incident."

"Incident? What incident?"

"Never mind that. How can I fix it? I feel so alone at home and I know that it should not be this way." I instantly knew that he was the last person I should be telling this to, but I needed some advice and I didn't have time to wait for a few therapy sessions or more. I was desperate for some help.

"Well ummm that depends on how you got there in the first place. How about we sit down over coffee or lunch tomorrow and discuss?"

"Uhhh---O-K, I guess." I really had not planned on seeing him just talking with him on the phone. The thought of seeing him made me a little nervous.

"Ok great, how about lunch? What time is your lunch break?" He inquired.

"At 12:30." I had to think of some place that I knew I wouldn't run into my husband. As innocent as my intentions were, I am sure he would not see it that way.

"Okay how about St. John's on Limerick St."

"Ok, sounds good and we can discuss some plans to reunite you with Alexis as well."

"Perfect!" He exclaimed with excitement.

I could not believe that I was planning to meet with him and discuss my marital problems. I must be desperate to talk with the man that put me through so much grief. Really what could my husband say about this anyway, he had already cheated and now he was shutting me out. I tried to talk to him, but he wasn't open to it so what else was I supposed to do? I was only trying to help our situation, not make it worse. I was not expecting what was to come.

I met with Kareem at St. John's at 12:35 as planned. He was there waiting on me at the table and had ordered two waters for us. As I approached the table, I felt a huge lump in my throat. I was nervous, a lot more nervous than I expected I'd be. He stood up to greet me. "Hey Alyssa! So glad you made it." He said as he reached out to hug me. I gave him a quick and innocent hug in return. Although, I had to admit, it felt good to be embraced. He pulled out my chair which made me reminisce on the gentleman he was when we were first met.

"Do you know what you want to eat? It's my treat of course."

I looked over the menu for a minute and answered "Yes, I think I'll have the southwestern chicken pasta"

He motioned for the waitress to come to the table and placed the order for both of us. We sat across from one another. It was a bit awkward for me at first. I could not help but notice Kareem was looking at me as if he were still in love with me, like he still wanted me. He was looking at me as if he knew that he had made a mistake in losing me. He was also looking as if, this was not a friendly sit down but a 'how can I get you back' sit down. "So, Alyssa tell me what's going on. We don't have a lot of time so let's just jump right to it. I want to help you in any way that I can. One thing is for sure, you are a woman that deserves to be happy."

"Thank you, Kareem". I say as I begin to blush.

"So, let's get to it, shall we? You know this is what I do now. Let me help you."

"Okay, so without getting into too many details, my husband has been isolating me. We don't have any interaction anymore."

"Okay, how long has this been going on?"

"For a long time now. Its taking everything from me now. I don't know how much more I can take. We are seeing a marriage counselor now, but it seems like it will take time to break some ground here and I am already over it." You could hear the frustration in my voice. It was almost as if I was giving up on my marriage.

"Maybe, I could help you work through this. You already have a marriage counselor, so I won't try to step in on that. I could help you work on some ways to handle this, but you would have to come to the office and you would have to be willing to open up about some of the things that have been going on between the two of you. Would you be willing to do that?"

"At this point, I am willing to try anything. You know me, I always said that once I get married, I want to stay married."

"Yes, I know, uh -um." He said as he cleared his throat. He began to look uncomfortable, but he tried to play it off.

"Ok, I can come to your office I suppose. How much would you charge me?"

"For you, I won't charge you a thing. It's the least I could do." He laughed.

"Wow okay, when can we get started?"

"Well, I have a full schedule everyday but if you can come in after hours I would be willing to see you then. It would probably be better to do it then anyway since it will be off the books. We can get started as early as tonight if you like, say around 7 pm?"

"Are you sure that this won't be a problem?"

"I'm positive. Just let me help you. Okay?"

"Okay, I will see you tonight at 7'o clock maybe a little after to give you time to clear the office. Last thing I want to do is get you in any trouble"
"Don't worry about me. I don't want you to get in any trouble with your husband."

"It will be fine, I will see if my mom can keep the kids for a while or I will tell my husband that I am going to see an individual counselor for myself. That is the truth!"

"Well now that we got that all settled. Where are we at with me seeing Alexis? Have you thought about it at all?"

"I did Jai—I mean Kareem." I said as I stuttered over my

words.

"J must be your husband?" He said with one eye brow raised.

"Yes, his name is Jaiden, sorry about that."

"You don't have to apologize."

"Alexis is young, it will be hard for her to understand that you are just coming back into her life. I agree that it does need to happen, you know that I would never intentionally keep you from her. I heard some rumors that you were telling people that I was keeping her from you is that true?"

He leaned back in his chair and confessed "Yes, at one point, I did say those things. I was wrong, and I owe you an apology for that. It was my way of convincing myself and others that I was not at fault, but the reality is, that I was. I know that now more than ever and I also know that the damage that I caused as a result is going to be difficult to repair. I learned a lot over the years and I have been enlightened in many ways. The situation with us is one of the main reasons that I chose to pursue marital and family counseling as a career. You and Alexis are the reason I turned my life around. I'm just sorry that I didn't do it sooner maybe then we....well never mind that."

"Kareem, I am glad that you got your life together and we will make this work where you can gradually pick up the pieces where you left off. We will figure it out and we will do it soon." I proclaimed.

"Well, it's time for me to get back to the office. I have clients coming in about 25-30 minutes." He said as he dropped the money on the table to pay for our lunch. We both got up at the same time.

"I have got to get back to work myself. I have clients to see too. I am in counseling myself, but I mostly work with children."

"I should have known, we always did have so much in common." He said as he gave me that killer smile.

"Thank you for lunch and I will see you later on this evening."

"I will see you then Alyssa."

We parted ways and I headed back to work. When I arrived back at work, I sent Jaiden a text that read: Hey I have an appointment with a therapist today at 7pm. Can you watch the kids until I get back?

Jaiden responded: I should be back in by 7:15 pm, I have an appointment that I need to go to today.

He did not disclose with me what it was that he had to do, nor did I inquire.

I texted back: Ok I will see if my mom can wait here with the kids for those few minutes until you get back.

He responded: Ok

That was that. I had everything lined up for our session tonight. I was curious and excited to get in and work on some of these issues with Kareem. He seemed to be very good at what he did. Only time will tell, if he would be able to give me the tools that I would need to fix my marriage. Clearly, I was desperate to have been relying on my ex for guidance in my current marriage.

After a long day at work, 5 pm finally hit and I was wrapping things up with my last client for the day. As soon as I was done I completed my notes and finished up my paperwork for the day. Around 5:45 pm I headed to before and after school care and picked up Alexis and JJ (Jaiden's son) was already at home. He was a latchkey kid. He could stay at home alone for a couple of hours. I left and picked Aniya up from daycare and headed back to the house.

I got home with Alexis and prepared dinner for the kids. I did not make myself any and Jaiden did not seem interested in eating my food lately, so I made just enough for the two of them. I made Aniya a bottle, fed a played with her for a few minutes. My mother arrived as scheduled at about 6:45 pm. I ran down some instructions with her and let her know that Jaiden should be home soon. I headed out the door for my meeting with Kareem. No way was I getting ready to tell my mother that I was meeting with Kareem. I don't think anyone would understand right now.

I pulled up to Kareem's office building at the address on his business card. The parking lot had just one car in it. A white newer model Honda Accord. I assumed it belonged to Kareem since he said that he would likely be there alone. I walked into the door and he was walking out of a door in the back "Hey Alyssa, I was just coming up to see if you had made it in yet? Let me lock this door behind you because we are officially closed."

"Hey"

Kareem walked up to the door and locked it as he announced, "Right this way ma'am". He waved his arms in the direction of his office. He was wearing a grey suit, with a very light lavender shirt and mauve colored tie. He was so handsome in his suit, but I wasn't there to admire his good looks. Frankly, I was feeling a little uneasy about being alone with him, but I knew my intentions were purely innocent.

He unbuttoned his jacket as he sat down in his executive chair. "Okay Alyssa, you have given me bits and pieces of the problem and I gather that you are uneasy about giving me too much detail so let's try this a different way. How about I ask you some questions and you answer them honestly? How does that sound?"

"Okay" I said hesitantly.

"How long have you been married to Jaiden?"

"We got married 2 years ago in August."

"How long did you date before you got married?"

"About a year and half." I answered.

"When did you start to have problems in your marriage?"

"I noticed a change in him almost as soon as we said, 'I do'. The real issues came in after about a year of marriage when I was 7 months pregnant with our daughter Aniya".

"Pregnant, you share a child?" Kareem said as he loosened his tie from around his neck. He seemed to get anxious about the news.

"Yes, we have a little girl now."

"Okay, so what happed while you were pregnant with Aniya"

"Well.... he cheated on me while he was away at a class." I said with vacillation.

"Wait, he cheated on you within a year of marrying you and conceiving a child with you?" I could see that Kareem was becoming infuriated with the information that I was sharing.

"Kareem are you sure you are going to be able to do this?" I inquired.

"Yes, I'm sorry…. yes", He declared as he sat up in his chair.

"Ever since that happened we haven't spoken, and he is sleeping in his 'man cave'. I don't know what to do. I feel rejected and lonely. I know I shouldn't be feeling this way but that's how he makes me feel. He didn't hardly utter a word when we went to counseling. He has an appointment next week by himself and I have one the week after next by myself. He just seems so distant and I am having a hard time finding ways to get him to talk to me. It's like we are roommates rather than husband and wife." Kareem seemed to be at a loss for words. He got quiet for a moment and put began to rub his chin as if he were pondering on an idea or thought. I was beginning to seriously question if Kareem could remain unbiased while he was working with me.

"Were there any red flags to alert you of this behavior?" He casually asks.

"Well not really but I guess we did move rather quickly and that was probably a red flag in and of itself."

"When you all were in a good place, what did you have in common?"

I thought for a moment as a long silence befell upon the room. "Well, only the fact that we were single parents." I responded.

"What does he do for a living?

"He's in the army."

"Say what? You have never been the type to deal with an army man. I remember your mother told me not to go into the military because you would leave me alone. She said you would never date a military man." He said as he chuckled a bit.

"Yes, I know but he seemed different for all the other military men that I had heard of. You know I have always thought that military men have a hidden agenda when they get into relationships."

"So, what made you think that he did not?"

"I don't know, to be honest all I ever did was compare him to you. He was opposite from you, so I thought that it meant that he would treat me better than you did."

"Oh God, I'm so sorry Alyssa. I can't apologize to you enough. I wish I could take all that hurt that I caused you back. He reached out to me and grabbed my hand.

"Listen, I want you to go home and try to talk to him tonight. Tell him how you feel being isolated and even if he doesn't respond, you will have gotten it off your chest. Let me know how the meeting goes and we will plan to meet again next week, same date, same time. How does that sound? If you need me before then, just give me call."

"Okay, Thank you. Thank you for listening to me. I know this is not easy for you given our history."

"No, it's not, but I am going to do my job to the best of my ability." He reached out to shake my hand.

"I'll see you soon." I said.

I NEED SOME SPACE

I planned to do exactly what Kareem said when I got home. However, I could not do it that night, it had to be well thought out and the timing needed to be perfect. Maybe Kareem was right. Maybe it was just that he didn't know that he was really hurting me by behaving this way towards me. I just needed to get it off my chest and maybe if Jaiden knew how badly this was hurting me he would be more inclined to fix it. I decided to wait until he went in for his individual session with Mr. Stanton.

I waited on that night all week and it had finally approached. I was anxious at work because I knew that I was going to have a very serious conversation with my husband and I was looking for a positive outcome. I marched into the house and checked on the kids. Alexis was in the bed sound asleep and Aniya was in her crib doing the same. JJ was in his room, so I didn't bother him. I went to Jaiden's door and knocked on it.

"Come in" he answered softly.

I walked into the room "we need to talk" I demanded. "I mean really talk, you know I say something and you respond."

"Okay".

"First off, how was your day?"

"It was good" he responded.

"Second, how was your session with Mr. Stanton?"

"It went well, I was able to get a lot of my chest." He remarked.

"That is great. Listen, speaking of getting things off your chest, I have a few things that I need to get off my chest as well. This distance between us is breaking me down. I am a married woman who is living in the same house as my husband but not in the same bedroom and I didn't do anything wrong. You said I didn't deserve what you did but, yet you isolate me. I wa---"

Jaiden cut me off "Listen Alyssa, I just needed some space. I needed some time to think about what happened. What I did to you. I never meant to hurt you. To be honest with you, I am not sure that I want to be married anymore."

"Wait what? You can't be serious right now!" I could not believe the words that were spewing from his mouth. I was trying to contain my anger, but this is one bold man first he comes home and tells me while I am pregnant with HIS child that he cheated then he casually says that he doesn't want to be married anymore. The nerve of this man. All I could think at this point was *who was this man that I am married to?*

"I'm sorry, it's not you it's me" he explained.

"So that's it, just like that, you want out?"

"Yes, I told Mr. Stanton today and he said that he will have a conversation with you when you come in for your appointment." He looked me straight in my eyes and said, "this was not meant to be."

What did he mean by that? How could he say these words to me? "What about marriage counseling, we are not going to give that a fair shot?"

"We did." He answered

"We only went to one session together, we were just getting started." I explained.

"I have made up my mind. I am done with this marriage. You deserve to be happy and so do I. Don't I?"

"What have I done to make you so unhappy Jaiden? You are the one that cheated on me."

"I told you, it's not you, it's me and I'm sorry I put you through all of this, but I feel it is better to end it now than to go further and deeper into this for the same outcome. Don't you agree?"

I was speechless, I could not respond. Did he not realize the severity of what he was saying? Did he think that a union was something that you just enter in and then casually opt out? Did he not remember the vows that he made to me? To my daughter? "What about our family?" I asked. As I recall he had asked the same question when he wanted me to forgive him for his infidelity.

"I will still take care of my child. I will pay you child support."

"Child support? What about all the other things that she will need from you besides finances, the emotional support, just you being there physically? What about Alexis? You made vows to her too, you know".

"Alyssa, you know that I am in the military. I will be moving from place to place. I won't get to see her that much, but I will do my best to spend time with her as much as I can. Alexis is your child not mine." He was so casual and calm as he explained this all to me. He picked up his keys and walked out. "I'll be back later" he comments.

I was completely distraught. In the blink of an eye, I was losing my husband and my oldest daughter was losing the only father that she has ever known and the daughter that we shared was losing her father. Pinch me, so I can wake up from this nightmare. After all of this we had come to the end of the road in our marriage and we were now firmly on the road to divorce. How was I going to break this to the kids? I needed some advice and I needed it fast and once again I could not wait a week to see Mr. Stanton. I called the only person that I thought could give me some support through this ordeal, Kareem.

"Hello" He answered.

"Kareem, I need to see you tomorrow evening if that is possible." I said as I let out a sniffle.

"Is everything ok? You sound upset. Did you talk to Jaiden about how you felt?"

"I tried to, but he wanted to talk about a divorce." I explained.

"Oh no, are you sure you want to wait until tomorrow, you can come to my place tonight or I can meet you somewhere." He offered.

"I can't, the kids are asleep, and I can't just leave them here." It was nice to know that he would jump to my rescue in a time of crisis though.

"I understand, I will be there. I actually had a cancellation at for my 6 o'clock, would you like to come in then?"

"Yes, that will work for me." I said with tears in my eyes. Kareem couldn't see the tears through the phone, but he could sense the sadness in my voice.

"I am sorry you are going through this, but we will get through it together, I promise. I will see you tomorrow."

I hung up the phone and laid it on my chest as I sprawled out on the bed. Things couldn't get worse than this.

BACK IN HIS ARMS

I had waited all day to meet with Kareem. I tried to keep myself busy at work. I think everyone knew that there was something wrong. I didn't have the energy to explain it to anyone nor did I want any of them to know my business. I only had one person at this job that I considered a friend but when she got married, she and her husband moved to a different area. Now, I work with a bunch of women who smile in your face and talk behind your back. The funny thing is, they talk about each other too. I have no patience for that type of pettiness at this stage in my life. I did not conduct myself in that manner, so I did not associate myself with anyone of them. I was not interested in having any of them in any part of my business. I kept to myself, did my work and went home.

I had already arranged for my mother to get my kids from school and daycare so that I could go and see Kareem and get some advice from him. They were set to spend the night with her. I knew that I would need some time to have some peace and quiet to process and make plans for everything that was getting ready to transpire. I was going to be off the next day and that would give me some time to just sit and think without having to deal with anything else.

As the time approached for me to leave, I began to feel a little anxious. I finished up with my clients a little early, so I decided to go home and shower just to help me relax some before I went to see Kareem.

As I pulled up, I saw the same lonely vehicle in the parking lot. When I approached the door, it was already locked. I guess that he had already shut everything down before I had arrived. I was running a bit late. I knocked on the door and I heard him unlocking it on the other side. He opened the door. "Hey Alyssa, come on in".

"Hey Kareem" I replied.

I walked in the door and we went to the back to his office. He closed the door behind us. "Have a seat on the couch, make yourself comfortable."

I sat down on the couch and it was if as soon as I hit the cushion a rush of emotions hit me. My eyes began to tear up and the realization hit me as to why I was sitting in his office in the first place. I reached for the Kleenex sitting on the table beside the couch and began to wipe my eyes.

"Tell me what is going on, Alyssa." He pleaded

"Well, I went home last night to talk to Jaiden about my feelings and he was so cold to me when he said that he just didn't want to be married. Can you believe he told me that it wasn't me it was him? Who does that in a marriage? How do you just wake up one day after reciting vows to someone, then doing all the dirt that he has done to me only to say I don't want to be married? I am so confused Kareem. I have done nothing to deserve this. I have been a good wife, he said so himself, yet he is just throwing me away like a piece of trash. What have I done to deserve this kind of pain?"

"Alyssa, you have done nothing at all to deserve this. You are a beautiful, educated, sweet, funny, and loyal woman. I could go on with the attributes, but you get the picture." He said as he rested his hand on my thigh. "I say this in the nicest way possible, but that man never loved you if he is willing to walk away without putting up a fight. Do you remember how much of fight we both put up? That is---- before I went too far with you that night?"

I listened intently as he went on.

"Alyssa you deserve the world and I wish I could have given it to you. I—I---just wish tha—never mind, I should not be saying that. This is my job I am here to help you with your situation it is so unethical for me to be discussing the past with you." He said as he put his head down as if he were ashamed.

"Go ahead Kareem, say what it is that you want to say. You wish that what?" I inquired.

"Well.... I wish that I would have gotten myself together and it was me that you were married to right now. You wouldn't be going through all of this and I hate seeing you like this. It hurts me to see you hurting. I will always have love for you. It was you that inspired me to be who I am today. I can't believe that you have had to go through all of this." He said as he shook his head.

I began to cry harder. I could not stop the tears. I couldn't help but wonder if any of this was my fault. If I was simply not worthy of being loved properly. This is all I have ever known in relationships. I have been cheated on, lied to, and just taken for a fool and no one including Kareem was willing to reciprocate the love I gave to them.

Kareem wrapped his arms around me as I cried. I laid my head on his shoulder. I extended my arms to hold onto him as well. There I was getting lost in his embrace again. I was even more vulnerable than I was during our last meeting. I felt a gentle kiss upon my neck that sent shockwaves through my entire body. *Did he just kiss me on my neck?* I thought to myself. It felt so good that I didn't want to push him away. He inched his way to my ear and whispered, "I'm still in love with you Alyssa".

I was having a moment of weakness. Vulnerability was oozing out of my pores. I had not felt this type of affection from a man in so long that the slightest touch made me melt. First the convictions began to swirl in my head. *What am I doing? This is so wrong. I shouldn't be here with him. Nothing good will come from this. I can't allow this to happen.* Yet, as every inch of body began to awaken as the heat radiated between my legs, I began to justify in my mind what was inevitably to come. *Well he is my first love. Jaiden did cheat on me with his co-worker. Technically, Jaiden is the one that ended things between us, and our marriage is over. This wouldn't be cheating. He is still so fine.*

I was completely lost in the moment and there seemed to be no turning back. It was like there was a fire inside of us that could only be extinguished with the connection of our bodies. I gave into his advances and before you knew we were passionately undressing one another. There was no denying that the chemistry between us was still there. That same intensity that we had when we were young and in love was still there. He lifted me up with those strong arms as his hands were planted firmly around my hips and my legs around his waist. He carried me over to his desk and held me effortlessly with one hand as he used the other to clear his desk. We began to extinguish the fire that was raging in us both.

I was feeling euphoric as if I was having an outer body experience. A feeling that I had not felt since he and I were in the early stages of our relationship. I desperately missed that feeling. The feeling of excitement and spontaneity. I was comforted by these feelings for a moment in time. All the hurt and pain that Jaiden made me feel had vanished in that moment. Kareem held onto me and would not let go. "Just like old times" he whispered in my ear softly.

Once I came down from that high, I begin to experience feelings of guilt and remorse. I had justified this one single action to gain momentary relief from the pain that was so deeply afflicting me. As I was getting dressed, I remember thinking, *what in the world have I done?* The feelings of regret were haunting me. *This is not me. This is not who I am.* I thought to myself.

As Kareem was tucking his shirt in, he could sense that something was wrong. "What's wrong sweetie?

"This was a mistake!" I quickly responded.

"Wait, a mistake? He asked as a look of bewilderment fell upon his face.

"Yes, a mistake Kareem!" I said in a slightly elevated tone.

"You think that us running into each other after all of these years during this time in your life and mine was a mistake? You think that it was by chance that we managed to avoid running into one another in the same town up until this point where I have gotten my life together and your 'marriage' is falling apart? This is something greater. This is God's plan for us. It may seem a bit unorthodox but you and I both know there is a reason that we were bought back together at this time."

"Brought back together? We are not together! Did you forget that I am still a married woman and you are a marriage counselor? You are supposed to fix marriages not tear them apart." I ranted.

"Now wait a minute, I didn't tear your marriage apart. It sounds to me as though you never had a real marriage in the first place. That man does not love you and if he did he would be willing to give your marriage a fighting chance not just throw in the towel because he's too lazy to put in the work. This isn't my fault!" He affirmed.

"You're right it's not your fault. It's my fault. I had no business here in the first place" I said as went to open the office door.

Kareem grabbed my arm before I could open it fully. "Come on Alyssa, you don't mean that. You just have a lot to contend with right now, but I told you I would be here for you and I will. I am just happy to have you back in my life and I am looking forward to the opportunity to have my daughter back in my life again".

"Kareem, I just need some time and space to process all of this, okay? I thank God for the changes that you have made in your life. I wish that you could have made them sooner but it's better late than never. But, you are right this is a lot to contend with and I am going to need some time to sort it out."

"Okay, I understand. Just know that I will be right here." He said as he watched me walk out the door. It was clear that he did not want me to leave. He followed behind me waiting for me to change my mind.

Once I got into the car and started on my way home, I rode in silence, no music, just me and my thoughts. There was a part of me that was hoping that Jaiden would be at the house waiting for me and I could go to him and say I slept with Kareem, just to hurt him the way that he had hurt me.

There was another part of me that was ashamed of myself for allowing this to happen. Although it was physically fulfilling it was mentally draining. *Is this how Jaiden felt when he cheated on me? Is that why he was so willing to reveal to me the truth in what he had done?*

Autumn Flowers

LIGHTS OUT

As I pulled up in the driveway, I noticed that Jaiden's car was not home. I press the garage door opener to park in the garage and it is not in the garage either. Something felt off, but I couldn't put my finger on it. I drove into the garage, parked my car, exited and lowered the garage door. As I opened the interior garage door which leads into the kitchen facing the living room, I notice that the big screen TV is missing off the wall. I began to panic, thinking that someone had broken in. I get my phone and type in the numbers 9-1-1 and held my phone tightly in my hand just in case I would need to get them on the phone in a hurry. I could not be sure that whomever had taken the TV off the wall was not still in my home. I walk through the house and peek in every room beginning with my daughter's rooms. Nothing had been disturbed.

I open my step son's door and his room was almost completely empty, everything was gone except the bed and dresser. I walked into Jaiden's man cave to find that it was empty as well, except for the big furniture. The only thing that stood in his room was a pool table and the futon bed that Jaiden had been sleeping on for months. It was at this time that I came to the realization that I didn't need the cops because my home had not been broken into. Jaiden had packed his things while I was a work and moved out of the house without so much as a warning or goodbye. Divorce was imminent. I realized that everything that Kareem said about Jaiden not ever loving me was true. So, *what were his true intentions with me?* I wondered.

The next few days were trying. I tried to call Jaiden, but he was not answering my calls. I had no idea how to reach him or where I could find him. Kareem tried to call me daily and I didn't answer his calls. I had way too much going on to take on anything else. He of all people should understand that. Nothing could prepare me for the turn of events that was getting ready to take place. As if I had not been through enough.

I had to go on with business as usual, I had two daughters that still needed me to be mommy. Jaiden had not even been in touch to check on his daughter Aniya, although she was way too young to even notice. Alexis was asking questions, hard questions and I had to give her hard answers. She took it awful hard and I could tell that she felt rejected. She couldn't express it in the most eloquent terms, but it was obvious. Kids are resilient and easily distracted, so it was not hard for me to take her attention and place it somewhere more positive, but it required a great deal of my own time and energy.

My appointment with Mr. Stanton was approaching and I could not wait to get in and process some of the things that had happened since our last visit, with him. I was sitting in my room while Alexis was taking a bath, writing some notes so that I would not leave anything out when I spoke to Mr. Stanton the following day. Aniya was sitting in her play pin playing with her toys. Suddenly, everything went dead at once. It was like a blackout. I heard my daughter Alexis scream out "Mommy". I jumped up and ran into the bathroom and she was scared because the door was closed, and she was in total darkness.

"Everything is okay baby let me help you get out of the tub." I helped her get out of the tub and wrapped her in a towel. I walked through the house flipping switches and everything was dead. The air conditioning had stopped too, and it was very hot out. I had just paid the light bill, so I knew that it was not a result of the power being disconnected for non-payment. I looked out the window at my neighbors houses to see if I saw any lights on in their homes, but it was too light outside to tell. I picked up the phone to call the electric company, it was entirely too hot to not have electricity. "Hello Johnson Power Company, this is Amanda, how can I assist you?"

"Hello Amanda, I was calling because my power is out in my home, is there some sort of outage in my area?" I inquired politely.

"I will be happy to look into that for you. May I get your address?"

"It is 8265 Heather Ridge Court."

"Thank you" She replied. I could hear her typing in the background. "Your name ma'am? She asked.

"Alyssa Williams" I replied.

"Mrs. Williams, I am showing here that Mr. Jaiden Williams called in a few days ago and requested to have the water and electricity disconnected on this date."

My heart sank. I could not believe what I was hearing. Not only could I not get in contact with him, but he has had the utilities disconnected in the middle of the summer while I have two children in the home to care for. I was having trouble understanding what would drive him to make such a cold-hearted decision.

"Hello, Ma'am are you still there?"

"Uh—uh yes I'm still here."

"He requested to have the final bill sent to 808 Rockingham Pl Apt C Spring Lake, NC 28348, Is this correct?"

"Uh, I'm sorry could you repeat that please?" I said as I grabbed a paper and pen to jot this address down. It may be my only lead to find out where he is.

"Yes ma'am, we have 808 Rockingham Place Apartment C Spring Lake, NC 28348. Would you like to make any changes?"

"Yes ma'am, both of our names are on this account, correct?"

"Yes ma'am, that is correct." She replied.

"Ok great, I would like to have the services reconnected. There will be no need to send a final bill to that address at this time. I apologize for any inconvenience." I stated politely.

"No problem ma'am, I will be happy to get that service reconnected for you. Unfortunately, because it is after 6 pm, we will not have any technicians available to get back out there until tomorrow."

I remained silent for a moment trying to process what she had just said. It certainly was not her fault and I did not want to take it out on her. I could feel my blood boiling and beads of sweat running down the center of my chest. I couldn't tell what was worse the rising temperature in the house or the fury that I was feeling causing my temperature to rise. "Uh yes, that will be fine, I guess, I don't have any other choice. Thank you for your help."

"Oh, you're quite welcome Mrs. Williams. Is there anything else I can do to assist you today?"

"No ma'am, thank you."

"Great, thank you for calling JPC and have a wonderful evening."

I wasn't sure how wonderful my evening could be with no electricity and no water for the evening and two children in the home. My main concern was for them. I had to make sure that they would be comfortable for the night which meant that I would have to take them somewhere else. The only place that came to mind was my parents and that would mean that I would have to give them the scoop on what had taken place between me and Jaiden. I wasn't ready to reveal that to them just yet but thanks to his actions, he left me no choice. I had nowhere else to turn, not anywhere that I felt comfortable staying with my children.

The amount of anger and resentment that I had towards Jaiden was mounting. I had what could potentially be his current address and I had to ponder on how I would use it to contact him. I didn't want to just pop up at his new place, if that is what this address was for but again he was leaving me no choice. I looked at my phone to see how much juice it had, and it was down to 15%, certainly not enough for me to try to call my parents and explain what was going on. No power meant that I had no way to charge it. I did however want to give them a heads up of my arrival. There was still some daylight, it really did not start getting dark until around 8 pm. That gave me a little time to get prepared to leave. I dialed my parents number and took a deep breath. I had to choose my words carefully or they would surely ask questions. I already knew that I would have to give a real explanation when we got there because Alexis would spill the beans as soon as she walked in the door. "Yello" My father answered, sometimes he would answer like that instead of saying 'hello' especially when he was in a good mood.

"Hey dad, what are y'all up to? I asked as I tried not to sound upset or bothered.

"Oh, nothing much, just sittin around watching T.V. I was thinking about getting a movie, but I know your mom isn't gonna watch it with me. Ya know she hates how loud it gets when I turn on the surround sound." He said as he chuckled.

"That sounds like fun, do you mind if me and the girls come and watch it with you?"

"No, no not at all. Come on. I'll see y'all when ya get here."

"Ok we will be there shortly. See you soon." I said as I disconnected the call.

I proceeded to gather our things while there was still enough daylight peeking through the windows for me to see. I placed our bags in the car and got the kids in the car. We traveled down the road as my parents stayed minutes from me. Once we arrived, I tried to mentally prepare myself for the mounds of questions that would be coming my way. Alexis hopped out and ran to the door screaming "Grandaddy!!!!" as my father greeted her.

"There's my girl". He said picking her up and spinning her around. They had a special bond, one that I admired. He had been that consistent male role model in her life.

"Granddaddy, our power went out when I was in the bathtub. I was scared." Alexis reported.

My dad gave me the side eye "oh really". He put Alexis down and said "Go ahead in the house and give your grandma hug. She is back there in the bed."

Alexis runs to the back as she was instructed to do. I carried Aniya back there so that my mom could love on her too. My mom spoiled them both. I walked back to the living room where my dad was sitting on the couch. "So, what's going on? Why are your lights out?" My father inquired. He had a look on his face as if he already knew that I had some bad news.

"Well, there's no easy way for me to say this so, I will just come out and say it. Jaiden and I are separated."

"Separated? When did this happen?"

"He left a few days ago and today he had the water and lights disconnected with no warning."

"He did what?" My father was getting excited, not the kind of excitement you have when you have just won something but the type of excitement that you get when you ready to knock someone's head off. "Let me get this straight, he left you and then left you in dark with no A/C on one of the hottest days this year, with two small children. What kinda man does that? Have you talked to him?

"No, he has not been answering my calls since he left, and I don't know where he is."

"You mean he hasn't even checked on the kids?" I could see the disappointment written on his face.

"Nope". I said as I broke into tears. I could no longer contain it. I was filled with so many emotions and it had all come to a head.

My dad reached out and hugged me. He could not stand to see me hurting. I knew that he had more questions, but he did not want to overwhelm me, so he refrained from asking. "Why don't you go lie down, your mother and I will make sure the kids get taken care of. It sounds like you have been through a lot."

I happily obliged. I was mentally and physically exhausted. I needed to rejuvenate my mind, body and spirit to be the best mother that I could be to my girls. I went to the back and laid down on my bed in my childhood bedroom. It was much different than it was growing up. When I closed my eyes, I could envision it exactly like it was when I was a kid. Instead I closed my eyes and fell into a deep sleep.

I DECLARE WAR!

I woke up well rested. My mother had already left to take Alexis to school and Aniya to daycare. I had no clients to see today and my job gave us the freedom to work from home on days like that. I did not normally opt to work from home, but under the circumstances I chose to utilize that option. I sent my supervisor a text to let her know that I would be working from home and to contact me on my cell if she needed anything. She responded "OK, make sure you get your notes to me by 3pm". I had my notes done yesterday, so that would be no problem.

I walked into the living room to find my dad sitting on the couch with his laptop in his hand. He was retired so it was not like him to be up and fully alert at this time of morning. "What are you doing up so early, dad?" I asked.

"I'm looking into a few things for you."

"A few things like what?" I asked with a look of confusion on my face.

"Well, I am researching the best divorce attorney's in the city. If he could treat you and the kids this way, there is no tellin what else he's capable of doin. Besides, there is no way you should let him get away with that."

"What do you mean dad?"

"You need to get you some legal separation papers and hold him responsible for leaving you and the kids in the heat.

There has got to be some kinda laws that protect you in situations like this and whateva they are I'm gonna find em."

"Dad, I can't afford a lawyer right now. I have the responsibility of taking care of all these bills on my own now. I've got car payment, utilities, rent, credit cards, daycare and the list goes on and on. Getting a lawyer is pricy and I would have to pay all that money up front."

"And that's exactly why you need a lawyer. Don't you worry about cost, it's on me. I know ya, I know ya didn't do anything to deserve this. I liked ol' Jaiden and I ain't never expect him to do this. But, you are my daughter and I will always support ya. This is what family does, we stick together."

"Thanks dad, but I don't know about this."

"Well listen, the offer is on the table. Think about it and let me know.

My dad always sprung into action whenever I was in trouble. It was nice to have that kind of support, but I didn't want this to get any uglier that it already had. It just was not my kind of thing. If Jaiden and I are going to get divorced, then I only hoped that our marriage would end amicably.

In that moment, I seemed to be the only one thinking that way because Jaiden would not even answer my calls let alone return them. Not to mention he left us in the dark on purpose. I wanted to keep myself busy until I was sure that the lights were back on at home and the house had an opportunity to cool back down. I asked my dad if he or mom could get the kids from school and daycare later because I had some errands to run and then I had an appointment with Mr. Stanton.

"Sure, why don't you just let us take them for a few days until you work some things out on the home front." He responded.

I hesitantly agreed because I hated being away from my kids especially when I was going through something. They were my solace. They gave me a reason to stay strong. However, I also needed some time to just be alone in my thoughts and really think about how I wanted to handle these issues.

I left the house and completed some errands which seemed to take up my whole day. Before I knew it, it was time to see Mr. Stanton. I had been waiting on this visit for what seemed like an eternity but really it was only a week. I walked into his office and checked in with the receptionist. A few moments later, he called my name "Alyssa, come on back."

I walked back into his office and sat down on the couch. "How are you doing today?" he asked.

"I've been better." I quickly responded.

"I'm sorry to hear that Alyssa. Do you want to talk about what's going on to make you feel that way?"

"I will get back to it, right now I would like to discuss your session with my husband. How did his individual session with you go? He said that he got a lot off his chest and he came to the realization that he didn't want to be married anymore."

"Well, ordinarily I would not be able to divulge this information with you, but he gave me express consent to not only speak with you, but he has also asked me to help you through this."

"Okay, how noble of him". I say as if I know what he is about to tell me.

"Well, we have a limited amount of time, so I will just dive right in." He said as he adjusted himself in his chair. "Jaiden shared with me that he no longer wanted to be married. That in fact, he never wanted to be married. He revealed that he only got married to you to get added benefits with the Army."

I was nodding my head as he spoke until he got to the part of about only getting married for added benefits from the Army. My face began to twist in bewilderment once he got to that part, but I couldn't utter a word."

"He revealed that he was never in love with you and that he thought that you felt the same. He said that he did not realize that you would take the marriage so literally and he felt it was best to get out of it now rather than to prolong it when he knew you did not want the same things."

"Wow, really?" I said in shock.

"I know that you are hurt and angry by this revelation but… may I be frank with you?"

"Of course, I prefer it that way." I said candidly.

"Uh-hmm…Within the first thirty minutes of talking to Jaiden, I knew that I didn't like him. He is my client or at least was--but he certainly rubbed me the wrong way. I have almost never experienced this with my clients. As he was making these bold statements to me I could see the emptiness within him. He was so cold and callous, narcissistic in fact. You however, I see the beauty in. You are a very attractive woman with many good qualities and you did not deserve to be mishandled in such a way. I just remembered our first meeting and how eager you were to repair your marriage, but he had a completely different agenda. I fully intend to help you get through this; I can only imagine the shock that you feel right now. You are strong and resilient; I know that you will not allow this defeat you.

Just like that, I had gone from marriage counseling to individual counseling. We continued our session until our time was up, but I was completely zoned out after learning that our marriage had been a sham. I reflected on how he had not only made vows to me but to my daughter and left not one dry eye in the church. *How could he say that he thought I knew?* I became infuriated that he had not only taken me through this but my innocent daughter who was so happy to have him in her life.

I wanted to confront him. I wanted him to face me and say these things to me. What kind of a man would stand behind someone else to reveal these things and then disappear...*A coward.*

Well there was no way that I was going to let him get away with this, he was going to have to face me like a man and tell me these things to my face. I needed an explanation for his actions. I pulled out the piece of paper that I wrote his forwarding address on as I walked out of Mr. Stanton's office. I typed the address in my GPS and I set out to get some answers. I would not have dared to tell Mr. Stanton of my intentions because I am sure that he would have done and said everything in his power to stop me.

As I pull up the address, I see two cars one belonging to Jaiden and the other, an unidentified vehicle that I had never seen before. It was a duplex the other car could have very well belonged to someone in the next apartment. I stepped out of the car and walked to the front door and tapped lightly. As I was standing on the front porch waiting for someone to come to the door, I noticed a package with the name Jovana Lopez.

For a moment, I thought I must be at the wrong house then a woman came to the door. I had seen this woman before. She was there when I initially picked Jaiden up from his tour overseas. Wait, could she be the co-worker he cheated on me with and if so just how long had it been going on and how serious was it? It was the woman who was staring at me when I picked up Jaiden from Green Ramp. She seemed to recognize me as well as she looked stunned that I was standing at the door. "J" she yelled out.

I could hear him in the distance "Yeah".

"You need to come here right now" she demanded.

"What's wro---" He said to the woman as he walked to the door and saw me standing there.

"What are you doing here?" He asked.

"A better question would be why did you leave me and

the kids in the dark with no water or lights without warning? Why did you bring another life into this world and drag me and Alexis through this mess knowing you had no intentions on being a husband and father? And is this the woman you cheated on me with? I asked as I pointed the woman.

She seemed as though she was embarrassed but she never spoke a word. She simply excused herself. Perhaps that was best.

"Alyssa, this isn't the time or the place."

"Oh yeah, you are not answering my calls. So, you are just going to abandon your responsibilities?

"You are no longer my responsibility." He said boldly.

"Seems like to me that you want a war with me. If it's a war you want, then it's a war you will get." I declared as I walked off with a smirk. Jaiden made no effort to stop me. He had no idea of the wrath that I was going to bring to him. In his mind he was probably thinking that I was going to ruin the items that he left behind in the house. He should have known better because that had never been my style. I had never been the vindictive type, but I was all about fairness.

I didn't want anything more than what the law would allow. Rest assured the judge would know all about the infidelity and his agenda that was revealed in therapy. They would also be made aware of how he had the utilities disconnected without warning while myself and the children were still living there. Let's not forget the fact that he has not even bothered to ask about his daughter. *Ughhhh!!!! What an asshole!!!* In an instant he had proven me right about military men with their hidden agendas.

I had seen and heard enough. It was obvious that I was not going to get any answers or explanations. It was equally obvious that he did not care about me or the kids. My dad had put that offer on the table about getting a lawyer and I could plainly see that he needed to be taught a lesson. He could not go around breaking women and children's hearts and not thinking twice about it. He needed to face some consequences and I intended to be the one to see that through. He showed no remorse and I was not going to have any mercy on him. I had planned to hit him where it hurt; his pockets.

Now everything that Kareem had been trying to convince me of about Jaiden not loving me and he and I not having anything at all had been confirmed. How could I have made such a huge mistake? I called my dad to confirm the that I wanted to go forward with the lawyer. "Yello"

"Hey dad."

"What's goin on baby girl?"

"Hey, I just wanted to let you know, I thought about the lawyer idea and I'm ready to proceed."

"10-4, I'll call the lawyers office in the morning and get you an appointment or you can do it yoself. If you're gonna do it, just make sure it's in the afternoon so I can go with you and take care of the payment for ya." He said with excitement.

"Okay, well I will wait on your call tomorrow. I will talk

with you then" I said as I hurried off the phone before I changed my mind.

Won the War, Still Lost

The day had arrived for me to go to the attorney's office. My father came along for moral and financial support. I walked into the office feeling nervous questioning if this was indeed the right the decision. I signed in with the receptionist and the attorney called me to her office shortly after. "Come on in Ms. Calloway" she said calling me by my maiden name.

I smiled and walked in the office and my father followed behind me. He did not say anything. I guess he just wanted to stay out of it as much as possible, so he just nodded and shook her hand. "I'm Rachel Loving's, attorney at law. So, what brings you in Ms. Calloway?"

"Well, my husband whom I am now separated from left me and the kids. When he left he had the utilities disconnected without giving us any warning and he has not been in contact with me to arrange visitation of any sort. While we were still together, he told me that he had cheated on me which is when all the problems began. I just want to know what I can do to protect myself and make sure that the kids are taken care of. What are my options?"

"Let me ask a question. Are you still in the marital home?"

"Yes ma'am."

"Okay, that's a plus, that indicates that he abandoned the marriage. Next, do you have any proof of his infidelity other than his word. Something like phone records, emails, text messages, pictures."

"I don't have any, but I can try to get my hands on something."

"Okay, the first thing we will need to do is file a legal separation, petition for equitable distribution, alimony, custody and child support. He does not get to walk away from a marriage as if it did not exist and certainly not the child that you share. He will have to own up to his responsibilities and it is my job to make sure he does. I have been doing this for almost 20 years, I have strong track record for getting results and this case seems to be pretty easy." She said very matter of fact and with confidence. I like that. She came off like she could be a real pit bull in the court room.

"Ok that sounds great, now can you explain what equitable distribution is?"

"Sure, it's basically splitting up the property and the bills that you shared as well as the marital assets. If you can get a hold of bank statements that show the amount that was in his bank account at the time of separation, then you are entitled to half of that. As well, he is to be responsible for half of any bills that you accumulated over the course of your marriage, so I will need that documentation. Because he abandoned the marriage for another woman, if you can prove it, you can sue for alienation of affection which is generally paid out monetarily."

"Wow. This all sounds good; how soon could we get this going and about how long will it take to resolve".

I can get the papers filed with the courts as early as tomorrow. It will take about 7 days from that date for him to be served with a court date. He will be given enough time to retain an attorney if he chooses but once we get a firm court date and a ruling is made in court, the order will take place immediately. I charge a $3000.00 retainer fee which generally covers everything unless we run into some complications which I don't foresee. If you are ready to start today, you just pay the retainer and sign an agreement with my paralegal and we can get the ball rolling."

"Awesome". It sounded simple enough. I just needed to go home and get busy gathering my evidence against him. One thing that everyone who knows me knows is that I can be inspector gadget when I want to be. I shook her hand and my father handed her a credit card to take care of the payment. We were all set. Jaiden would never see this coming. This ought to teach him to underestimate me.

"I will be in touch with you as soon as I get any new info. My paralegal Latosha Sanders will be your best point of contact if you need anything or have any questions. We are all set!" Ms. Loving's said as she walked us back to the front.

I walked out of her office feeling protected. I felt assured that Jaiden was going to get what he deserved for what he had done to me and the girls. He had done the unthinkable and dragged me through the mud but in that very moment, I knew that I would knock him off that high horse.

I went home and started to do my P.I. work. I pulled up phone records and bank statements. I found bank statements showing that he had 250,000 in a bank account. It was part of money that he had received when his mother passed away, shortly after we were married. He never mentioned any settlement to me and I was completely unaware of this large lump sum of money.

I even gained access to his email and much to my surprise an email stuck out like a sore thumb. The subject line read: How could you do this to me. It was dated 10/21/2010 which was shortly after we were married. It read: Jaiden,

Now that I see what type of man you are, I want nothing to do with you. You had me sitting here waiting on you while you were in Iraq like you asked me to. I did it because I loved you and I thought that you loved me too. I was wrong. I am so glad that I lost the baby that I was carrying. I can see that you would not have been a good father anyway. I hope you go to hell!

Vicki Brower

I opened his reply to her email and it read. Vicki,

I'm sorry that I hurt you. I just don't feel like we were right for each other. I wish you much success and I hope we can still be friends.

Love always,
Jaiden

My eyes almost popped out of my head they got so big. I was in shock. What else was he up to? Seemed to be that I was not the only woman he had schemed on. I just happened to be the unlucky one who married him. I hit the print button and filed it in my folder of evidence against him. Of course, this email prompted me to dig a little deeper because this email was not from Jovana Lopez, the woman he cheated on me with and that is what I was looking for. Low and behold, I found bunch of similar emails from a bunch of other women to include nude pics. Jack pot! I was no longer doing this just for me and my kids. I was doing this for the countless other women that he had victimized. I gathered enough evidence to show that he had unfaithful throughout the course of our marriage with many different women. It was enough to win the case that I had pending against him. It was also gut wrenchingly painful to discover.

I forwarded mounds of evidence and documentation to my lawyer and waited for her to make me aware of the court date. About two weeks later, I started to get calls from Jaiden. I mean he was blowing my phone up, I guess he had been served. I decided to pay him the same respect he had been paying me. I didn't answer! He called one last time and left me a voicemail "So you are taking me to court huh? You can have the baby, but you won't get anything else. I'm only going to give you $400 a month in child support, that's all I have left after I pay my bills. You're a bitter bitch for doing this but you won't win. I have already spoken to JAG and they have advised me on what to do" He let off this sinister laugh and then hung up.

What was sad was that he didn't think anymore of the child that he helped bring into this world, my daughter. He was blatantly ready to abate his responsibilities as a father. My heart ached for my daughter who would one day grow up to realize that her father openly abandoned her. But his ideals about how marriage, family and divorce worked were largely flawed. What in the world made him think that he would only have to pay me $400.00 per month? What in the world was JAG going to do for him in a civilian courtroom? He had no idea what kind of shit storm I was going to bring his way but with the way that he was behaving and treating us, it made it easy for me to do.

Over the next couple months, the stress surrounding the court case was unimaginable. I lost weight, I lost my hair and it felt as though I was losing my mind. We finally had our day in court and the anticipation of the outcome was taking its toll on me. When the judge called our names, I went and sat beside my lawyer on one side and he went and sat by himself on the other side. Rachel whispered in my ear "don't worry this won't take long, he doesn't have an attorney, he is representing himself." The bailiff announced "All rise, court is now in session. The Honorable Judge Geraldine McLeod is presiding." The judge entered the courtroom as we all stood. Then the bailiff announced, "you may all be seated."

Judge McLeod called Jaiden to the stand and asked him bluntly "Young man, do you wish to represent yourself?"

He responded, "Yes ma'am I do, I have been advised by legal counsel on how to handle the proceedings."

"Are you sure that is what you wish to do? You do realize that once these proceedings are final that you will not be able to readdress the matter."

"I do your Honor?"

"Very well." She said. "Bailiff take Mr. William over there to sign a waiver". Jaiden walked up to the stand and signed a document and the proceeding were ready to begin. "Mrs. Loving's would you tell us what your client is petitioning for today?

"Yes, Your Honor, my client is petitioning for sole custody of their daughter Aniya Williams, Child support in the amount of $1204 per month and $1660 in Alimony for the next 18 months." Judge McLeod was writing everything as Rachel was talking and Jaiden was snickering to himself. "My client would also like to establish equitable distribution. She would like to keep the marital home, the vehicle that they purchased together, and half of the assets acquired over the course of their marriage in the amount of $125,000."

"What?" Jaiden shouted

The judge tapped on her gavel twice "Mr. Williams please remember that you are in a court of law. I will give you an opportunity to speak." She said as she addressed Jaiden. She then looked at Rachel "On what grounds are you requesting Alimony payments counsel?"

"Your Honor, Mr. Williams abandoned the marriage and the child. He also had extra marital affairs throughout the marriage."

"Is there any proof of said affairs?"

Rachel approached the bench with a folder containing the evidence along with my cellphone in which she played the voicemail of Jaiden saying that I can have the baby. *What a huge mistake that was!* Judge fumbled through the documentation expressionless for about 15 minutes. She then called Jaiden to the bench "Mr. Williams please approach the bench." Jaiden walked briskly and confidently to the bench. I guess he thought that wearing his military uniform displaying all his medals and awards was going to leave some type of positive impression on the Judge. "What do you have to say about this voicemail?" Judge McLeod inquired.

"I was just upset, Your Honor."

"Did you ever tell your then wife about this check that your received for $300,000 when your mother passed?"

"No ma'am I did not." He hesitantly replied.

"What is it that you think that Mrs. Williams deserves from you to continue supporting the kids?".

"Well Your Honor, I was told by JAG that my financial obligation for child support would be $400.00 per month and I am willing to give her that."

"How generous of you Mr. Williams however you were not advised properly by JAG. You probably should have been represented by an attorney. I am not sure how much that would have helped you considering the evidence against you. Your behavior over the course of this marriage is grossly egregious and your lack of concern for your young daughter is iniquitous. As such, it is my ruling that Mrs. Williams or Ms. Calloway, (as I am sure she would prefer to be called by her maiden name), be awarded full custody of the child in question. You have made no effort to contact this child since you have separated, and you clearly stated your feelings in the voicemail that I heard. Her request for child support and alimony have been awarded."

Jaiden cut Judge McLeod off "that is over half of my pay, I" Judge McLeod then cut him off "Mr. Williams, another one of those outbursts and I will hold you in contempt. As I was saying, the alimony is being awarded due to the extra-marital activity that is evident. It is obvious that you are at fault for the marital dissolution therefore you are going to pay Ms. Calloway to make sure she can maintain the same lifestyle for the next 18 months. Also, I am ordering you to pay Ms. Calloway 125,000 of the money that you have in savings. The money that you intentionally tried to hide. That money is to be paid to her in the form of a certified check no later than 10 days from today's date.

If you would like to arrange visitation, I will leave that open for 90 days and you can request through the child and family mediation services before then. Are there any questions? She asked.

"Yes, how will I pay my bills?"

"Well, Mr. Williams you should have thought of that before you stepped out on your marriage. Just be glad that Ms. Calloway was nice enough not to come after the woman too for alienation of affection. Have a nice day Ms. Calloway and you too Mr. Williams." She tapped her gavel once and waited for us to dismiss.

Yes! I had won my case against him. Initially I was ecstatic about my win against him. It felt good to stick it to him and see him suffer the consequences of his actions. I walked out of the courtroom with a huge grin on my face and a weight lifted off my shoulders. As the day progressed that happiness shifted to emptiness.

Money was not going to solve my problems. I still had two daughters at home that didn't have a relationship with their fathers. I was a single mother with two children with two different fathers. I was seeking the same type of comfort from both of them. The more I thought about how I had fallen back into the arms of Kareem for that brief moment, the more I realized that I never really loved Jaiden myself. I wanted the family unit like I had grown up watching on the

Cosby Show and I was willing to ignore the red flags to get it. I guess you could say that I had a hidden agenda of my own.

You see, we all have our motives for the things that we do in life some good, some bad, some intentional and some unintentional but the fact remains that there is always a reason.

I now had a great deal to overcome and there was no amount of money could fix it. I had to do some serious introspection and really get to the heart of why I made the choices that I made that brought me to this point in life. This chapter with Jaiden is closed. As for Kareem......only time will tell.

www.ingramcontent.com/pod-product-compliance
Lightning Source LLC
Chambersburg PA
CBHW050042180626
46810CB00002B/848